LUCY DANIELS

Polars
— on the —
Path

Illustrations by Ann Baum

Hodder
Children's
Books

a division of Hodder Headline Limited

Special thanks to Ingrid Maitland

Thanks also to C.J. Hall, B.Vet. Med., M.R.C.V.S., for reviewing the veterinary information contained in this book.

Animal Ark is a trademark of Working Partners Limited
Text copyright © 2002 Working Partners Limited
Created by Working Partners Limited, London W6 0QT
Original series created by Ben M. Baglio
Illustrations copyright © 2002 Ann Baum

First published in Great Britain in 2002
by Hodder Children's Books

For more information about Animal Ark,
please contact www.animalark.co.uk

10 9 8 7 6 5 4 3 2 1

A Catalogue record for this book is available from the British Library

ISBN 0 340 79552 2

Typeset by Avon Dataset Ltd, Bidford-on-Avon, Warks

Printed and bound in Great Britain by
Clays Ltd, St Ives plc

Hodder Children's Books
a division of Hodder Headline Limited
338 Euston Road
London NW1 3BH

POLARS ON THE PATH

Mandy was thrilled to be this close to the polar bears, but she knew that the mother would be feeling very frustrated and desperate to protect her cubs.

The polar bear stood on her hindlegs. Her head swayed from side to side and she showed her teeth in a low grumbling growl. Mandy could feel the hairs on the back of her neck stand on end. She was amazed at how brave John Bruce was. The huge bear stared directly at him, perfectly balanced on her back legs, but he slowly raised the tranquillising gun to his shoulder and peered along the barrel, aiming for the bear's chest.

Suddenly, one of the cubs decided to run for it. It seemed to Mandy that the mother bear was trying to weigh up whether to go after it, or stay and confront the humans threatening the remaining cub.

But she didn't get a chance to decide. Mr Bruce found his mark through the falling snow – and fired.

Animal Ark series

Plus:
Little Animal Ark
Animal Ark Pets
Animal Ark Hauntings
Animal Ark Holiday Specials

One

'I feel like an elephant in these clothes!' Mandy Hope looked at her reflection in the mirror and laughed. 'I'm three times my normal size.'

There was little to be seen of Mandy's legs. The enormous padded parka she wore hung to her knees. She had stuffed her fleece-lined trousers into a pair of thermal socks and pulled on chunky snowboots.

'You'll be *warm*,' her mum told her with a smile, 'and that's all that matters when you're out there!' She pointed towards the window in their hotel bedroom. Mandy flexed her toes inside the fur-lined boots and walked heavily across the room to look out. She saw the sun shining on a dazzling white, barren landscape, which spread away from the main street of the small Canadian town. Instead of cars, sleighs and snowmobiles made up the main Saturday morning traffic, and everyone was wearing the same oversized padded clothes to protect them from the cold.

Mandy could hardly believe she was here – in Churchill, Manitoba, just a few degrees south of the Arctic Circle. Most exciting of all, this was a region in which Mandy knew she would be certain to see one of her favourite animals – the polar bear.

Mandy had been on the lookout for polar bears ever since they had landed at the military training ground that served as Churchill's tiny airport. As they had taken the bus into town, she'd seen several roadside signs warning visitors to watch out for the white bears, as they could be dangerous: DON'T GET OUT OF YOUR CAR! DON'T WANDER OFF THE ROAD! The signs were written both in English and in Cree, a Native American language.

Mandy turned to her father. He was sitting at a

writing desk, studying an article on polar bears in a wildlife magazine. She leaned over his shoulder and admired a photograph of a mother bear lounging on the ice with her cubs peeping round her massive body. 'So why exactly do the polar bears come to Churchill?' Mandy asked.

Adam Hope took off his reading glasses. 'Well, the town is on the western edge of Hudson Bay,' he explained. 'Now that it's October, the bears are waiting for pack ice to form on the bay so they can go out and hunt seals for the winter. They've made their way here from their summer dens further inland. The urge to go out on the ice is so strong that sometimes they arrive here weeks before the water freezes over.'

'But I thought polar bears could swim,' Mandy said. 'Why don't they just jump into the bay to hunt?'

'Seals are much faster swimmers than bears!' Mrs Hope laughed. 'They'd never catch them.'

'Polar bears are very skilful creatures,' Mandy's dad told her. 'They know that the seals are under the ice, but they also know that the seals have to come up to the surface to breathe oxygen. So the bears wait beside the breathing holes. And when the nose of a ringed seal appears, they grab it with a mighty claw – and there's lunch.'

'We really *will* see polar bears, won't we?' Mandy had asked this question many times already. She couldn't quite believe that she was about to come face to face with one of the world's most amazing creatures.

'Churchill isn't called the polar bear capital of the world for nothing, love,' said Mrs Hope, ruffling the fur trim framing Mandy's face.

Mandy took up her vigil beside the window once again. She was starting to feel really impatient. She peered through a patch of melting snow which was packed against the window. Even in the heated hotel room, the pane was icy against her nose. 'Is it nearly time to go, Mum?'

'Nearly,' Emily Hope confirmed. 'The man at the reception desk will let us know when the tundra buggy arrives to take us out to the bears.'

Mandy's parents were both vets. They had come to Churchill at the invitation of a Canadian university to do some research into the effects of tourism and climate change in the Arctic and sub-

Arctic regions. It was going to mean six weeks away from their home in Welford, Yorkshire, where the Hopes ran the Animal Ark veterinary surgery.

Mandy's school had agreed to her being away, as long as Mandy promised to complete some schoolwork assignments, and kept them informed of all her exciting experiences. It was just another part of the adventure Mandy was looking forward to – writing to her friends at home and telling them about life in the far, frozen north. Mandy grinned as she pictured her best friend, James Hunter, and his lively labrador Blackie. What were they doing now?

The shrill ringing of the telephone startled her. She sprang from the window and snatched it up. 'Hello? Mandy Hope speaking,' she said.

'The tundra buggy is at the front of the hotel now, Miss,' said a friendly voice.

'Thank you!' Mandy replied. 'We'll be down in a moment.' She replaced the receiver. 'It's here! Come on Mum, Dad. Hurry!'

Moving quickly in clothes so thickly insulated really wasn't easy, Mandy thought again, as she shuffled into the hotel lobby. A man in a dark blue padded jacket was herding tourists out of the front door and down the steps to the waiting buggy.

Mandy couldn't help grinning when she saw the buggy. 'It looks like a school bus on tractor tyres!' she pointed out, gasping as the icy air reached her lungs. The buggy was high off the ground, high enough to stop the bears from sticking their heads in, even when standing on their hindlegs. The giant tyres allowed it to travel across the icy and difficult terrain.

'Look at the sealed windows!' Mr Hope remarked. 'They're there to protect people from the paws of hungry bears.'

'Oh, wow!' Mandy exclaimed.

'Well, I just hope it's heated,' Emily Hope muttered, pulling her scarf up over her chin.

A steel ladder had been lowered from the rear of the buggy to the ground. As Mandy clambered up, gripping the metal railing with her hands in their thick mittens, she saw a raised, open-air platform on the back. It was like a balcony, with room for about half a dozen people.

'That's good,' said Mr Hope, also noticing the

balcony. 'We should get some great photographs from up there.'

A little shiver of excitement raced up Mandy's spine. She took a seat in one of the rows inside the buggy, squeezing in between her parents. When the other passengers were settled, the buggy started up. Its large wheels began to churn slowly across the ice.

Soon Mandy could feel welcome warmth round her ankles, generated by the buggy's engine. As they motored along the main street, Mandy was amazed to see how desolate Churchill appeared. It was an isolated Arctic outpost where no roads led to the outside world, and it boasted just seven hundred inhabitants.

The buggy left the town behind and headed east across the tundra, to the shores of Hudson Bay. Mandy became aware of a peaceful silence. She twisted sideways and gazed out of the window at the great expanse of frozen wasteland, the sub-Arctic tundra.

'Does the ice ever melt?' she asked, curious about this alien landscape. 'Is there any grass underneath it?'

'The surface of the tundra melts each summer,

but the ground below stays frozen all year round,'
Adam Hope told her. 'It's called permafrost.'

'Have you noticed how few trees there are,
Mandy?' Mrs Hope asked. 'That's because trees
can't sink their roots into ice. The caribou have
to live off the moss and lichen, which have much
shorter roots.'

The buggy continued slowly along the shores
of the bay. Mandy looked out at the fog hanging
in a cloud above the snow. She knew that this
blanket of ice stretched all the way up to the North
Pole. And that animals living here, like polar bears
and caribou, a type of reindeer, had adapted to
some of the most inhospitable conditions in the
world.

Suddenly, a voice disturbed Mandy's thoughts.
'I see one!'

Mandy jumped out of her seat and looked to
where a man was pointing. Ambling along the
snow towards them was a huge, lone bear. In the
wintry sunlight, his coat looked a lemony yellow
colour. He made straight for the bus, lifting the
black button of his nose to sniff the air.

Mandy stood up in her seat to get a better view.
The bear padded closer, the curved black claws

on his toes clearly visible. There was a scramble for cameras all around.

The driver opened the windows in the ceiling of the buggy. Mandy was just tall enough to look out over the rim of the bus's roof. 'He's gorgeous!' she whispered, not wanting to frighten the bear.

'He's *huge*,' Emily Hope said softly.

'They're not afraid of us,' said the driver at Mandy's elbow, in a loud and cheerful voice. 'They're used to humans now.'

'Really?' Mandy asked, not taking her eyes off the polar bear. 'How come?'

'Not long ago, Churchill was a place nobody visited. It was only used as a seaport for the Arctic,' the driver explained. 'Then a local man came up with the idea of these vehicles. It meant people could travel safely across the tundra to watch the bears. Since then, every year around September, the town is packed with tourists wanting to see the bears migrate.'

'So that's why the polar bears are used to people?' Mandy asked him, craning her neck as the bear stooped to sniff at the wheels of the buggy.

'Very much so!' he said. 'The buggies used to bring food, but we don't allow people to feed them any more. We don't want the bears to rely on humans for food.'

As Mandy watched, the polar bear stood up on his hindlegs, and looked in at the faces staring back at him. There were gasps of surprise and fear as people pulled back from the windows. Mandy felt her skin tingle with excitement. The bear was close enough for her to see his sharp canine teeth and dark pink tongue. His warm breath made a cloud in the freezing air. He shuffled about on his back feet, as big as soup plates, then dropped gracefully to the ground.

'He must be cold,' Mandy said, watching the biting wind ruffling his long fur.

'I shouldn't think so.' Adam Hope shook his head. 'Polar bears are perfectly adapted to this climate, Mandy. This chap has a thick layer of fat and insulating fur to keep him warm.'

'Polar bear fur is translucent, which means light can get through it. Each hair reflects heat from the sun down to the base, where it is absorbed into the bear's special black skin,' Emily Hope added.

'Do they eat moss and lichen like the caribou

when the bay is frozen?' asked Mandy, surveying the bleak landscape. A few scrubby, stunted bushes clung to the ice, but they didn't look very appetising.

'They might do,' the driver replied. 'But they don't eat that much in the summer months. They live off the fat reserves that they built up over the winter. It means that right now, at the end of the summer, they're pretty hungry!'

A buzz of excited chatter alerted Mandy to something going on at the front end of the buggy. Standing on tiptoe, she saw two bears rolling and tumbling about on the ice.

'Look! Mum, Dad!' Mandy pointed and Mr and Mrs Hope hurried forward. The bears looked as if they were fighting. They stood up on their hindlegs, their front paws paddling comically, then they raced towards each other at a furious speed. Mandy held her breath as their great furry bodies collided and crashed into the snow.

'It's as though they're putting on a show for us,' said Emily Hope, laughing.

Mandy was amazed. 'But are they really fighting?' she asked.

'No, just playing,' answered the driver. 'They

don't need to fight for dominance or for females at this time of the year. But play-fighting gives them a chance to practise their skills, ready for when they do have to fight.'

Mandy felt as if she could have watched for hours, but the bears soon tired of their game and ambled away. The driver started up the buggy and headed for their midday stop, where they would be having lunch. After about half an hour, they drew up beside a specially-designed stationary 'tundra train'. It was painted red and raised high above the tundra on huge wheels. Three carriages had been turned into a restaurant. There were bunk beds in the last carriage, for tourists who wanted to stay overnight.

Groups of bears prowled at a distance, watching the tourists arrive.

'There are loads of them!' Mandy joyfully exclaimed.

'They can smell the food in the kitchen,' the driver explained.

'Hmm, so can I!' said Mr Hope, as he descended the buggy ladder. 'The cold certainly gives you an appetite!'

They were ushered the short distance from the

tundra buggy into the train by a man who was armed with a tranquilliser gun. He kept a wary eye on the pacing bears.

'Vegetable chilli!' Mrs Hope said approvingly, as Mandy came up on to the top step. She was peering into a steaming dish on a buffet table in a dining-room.

'Oh, great,' Mandy grinned. She started peeling off her coat and scarf. It was warm and snug in the long, narrow room.

Mrs Hope sat down next to the window. 'What a view!' she said, gazing out across the endless flat scenery.

'I must be dreaming.' Mandy laughed, joining her. 'How can I be watching polar bears in the wild while having lunch?'

Fresh snow on the icy landscape showed the giant paw marks of the polar bears. One large bear was stretched out on his side, snoozing, as though soaking up the sun on a beach. Three others stood looking at the tundra train with alert, watchful faces. They sniffed continually, their noses twitching, testing the air for the scent of food. Mandy watched, spellbound, as two of the smaller bears played a game of catch, scattering snow with their paws as they leaped in circles. By accident, one of them skidded into the slumbering giant, who responded by showing them his huge teeth, and swatting at them with a front paw. But then he got up and plodded away to find a safer spot to sleep, shaking the loose snow from his coat with a shrug of his massive shoulders.

It was hard to believe polar bears were among the world's most dangerous carnivores. They looked so cuddly, Mandy thought. She could have spent the rest of the day just gazing out at them, watching them waddling round on their furry hindlegs, blinking their beady black-button eyes and twitching their shiny noses. But all too soon, their driver called out for his party to return to the buggy. It was time for the hour-long journey back into Churchill, along the misted, frosty shores of Hudson Bay.

Two

By the time the tundra buggy pulled into Churchill, the snow-laden skies had darkened to dusk. The town had a festive feel to it. Carved faces on candlelit pumpkins grinned out at Mandy from most of the shop windows, as she set out again from the hotel with her parents. On the following day, they were going to stay with John Bruce, a local wildlife officer, and his family. Mandy's parents had been put in touch with Mr Bruce by the university that was sponsoring their research. Tonight, the Hopes were going to meet the Bruce family for the first time.

'Hallowe'en!' Mandy cried, stopping to admire a ghastly, green ghost mask.

'Not quite yet,' Adam Hope said. 'A couple of days to go. Now, we ought to get going if we want to be in time for dinner with the polar sheriff!'

'The polar sheriff?' Mandy echoed. 'What does he do?'

'He's not a real sheriff,' her mother explained, linking arms with Mandy as they picked their way along the icy pavement. 'He's what they call a natural resource officer. He works closely with the research station in Churchill. Scientists are able to study the bears round here very closely, because there are so many of them. The bears are caught using a tranquillising dart from a special gun, which puts them to sleep for a bit. Then the polar bears have identity tags punched into their ears.'

Mandy frowned. 'Doesn't that hurt them?'

'Not really,' Adam Hope assured her. 'It's just like having your ears pierced. It's so that when the scientists recapture them later, they can work out how far the bear has travelled and make a note of any changes in weight and condition. It really is the best way of finding out about their life on the ice.'

'Is Mr Bruce a scientist, then?' asked Mandy.

'No.' Mr Hope shook his head. 'His job is to look out for the bears and keep them out of the town. After all, polar bears can be dangerous, like all wild animals. Even if they do look sweet and fluffy!'

Mandy nodded happily. She couldn't think of a more exciting job than to be a polar sheriff. She felt lucky to be in Churchill and was about to say so, but her face felt numb with cold, and snowflakes kept settling on her mouth and nose, so she kept quiet and concentrated on where she was putting her feet. They had walked about half a mile along the main street, stepping carefully on the treacherous pavement. There were a few small commercial buildings along the side of the road, and rows of houses propped on sturdy wooden stilts, to keep them off the ice. All of the shops sold arctic winter wear, and general provisions, and most of them made some reference to the polar bears. Mandy lost count of the number of stuffed toy polar bears she saw, grinning out at her from shop windows. She could see why the toys would be very popular with tourists.

'This is it, number 43.' Adam Hope pulled his arm free from Mandy's to unlatch a wrought iron gate. Beyond was a flight of steps to a red door.

'Thank goodness we're here.' Emily Hope banged her gloved hands together. 'I'm so cold!'

The door was opened by a big man with a bushy brown moustache. Behind him was a tall dark-haired girl.

'Come in! Come in!' John Bruce drew them indoors with a booming welcome. 'Adam and Emily Hope and . . . ?' He raised his eyebrows. Mandy was surprised to hear that he had a Scottish accent.

'Mandy,' she said with a smile, as Mr Bruce shook her hand warmly.

'This is Alicia, my daughter,' Mr Bruce said. 'My wife, Grace, is at work but she'll be home a little later. She's looking forward to meeting you. Come on in.'

'Hello,' Mandy said to the tall girl hovering behind her father.

Alicia said hello, then bent to scoop up a Scottie

dog that had come trotting into the hall to meet the visitors.

Mandy's eyes lit up. 'Oh, how sweet! Is he yours?' She reached out to stroke the dog's fuzzy black head.

'Yes. This is Hamish,' Alicia told her. Hamish waggled his stumpy tail and licked Mandy's fingers. Because of the snow and the polar bears, this tiny pet dog was the last thing Mandy had expected to find in Churchill.

Alicia led Mandy into a big room that served as a living-room and kitchen. Mr and Mrs Hope were already warming themselves beside the electric fire. Coats, hats, gloves and scarves lay in a heap on a table at the edge of the room. Mandy slipped off her boots and added her own coat to the pile. John Bruce was pouring hot chocolate into mugs. A delicious smell filled the room.

'It's a relief to be indoors!' Emily Hope took off her knitted hat and shook out her long auburn hair.

'It's only minus eleven out there,' Mr Bruce said cheerily. 'When it gets to minus fifty, then you're talking cold!'

Mrs Hope gave a shudder.

'So, what brought you to Churchill in the first place?' Adam Hope asked their host.

'I came on a secondment from the Scottish police force, just over fifteen years ago,' Mr Bruce explained. 'I met Alicia's mother, and stayed.'

'It's a fascinating part of the world,' Mandy's dad said enthusiastically.

'And we've already seen some polar bears,' Mandy added.

'Aren't they fantastic?' Alicia exclaimed. 'I never get tired of watching them, and I've got loads of photos. Would you like to see them?'

Mandy nodded. She could tell that Alicia was mad about animals, just like her.

'Let's take our drinks upstairs,' Alicia said. 'Follow me.'

Alicia's small bedroom was reached via a steep wooden staircase. It had a sloping ceiling adorned with hundreds of photographs of polar bears. Some had been cut from magazines, but others had been taken with a camera. Mandy felt instantly at home, and couldn't help being impressed by the photos Alicia had taken. Some of the shots looked as if she had been really close to the bears.

Mandy sat on Alicia's bed, looking around her. As well as photography, Alicia was clearly a keen reader. There were books everywhere – stuffed into the rafters, on shelves, and peeking out from underneath the bed. Most of the titles had something to do with animals.

'What do you think of Churchill?' Alicia asked her, taking a sip of her hot chocolate.

'It's wonderful!' Mandy's eyes were shining. 'What an amazing place to live! We went out in the buggy to see the bears near Cape Churchill

this morning, and I couldn't believe how many we saw!'

'You've certainly come at the right time of year to see them,' said Alicia. 'The only thing that outnumbers the bears right now is the tourists!'

Just then, Hamish jumped up on the bed and curled into a ball beside Mandy. She stroked his soft black fur. 'Doesn't Hamish feel the cold?' she asked.

Alicia shook her head. 'He wears a coat when he goes out for a walk. I have to be very careful taking him out at this time of the year. While the polar bears are about, Hamish would make a very tasty snack!' She smoothed his coat lovingly.

'Are they really dangerous?' Mandy asked. 'The bears, I mean. They look so . . .'

'They can be nuisance – but only when they're hungry,' Alicia told her. 'I think the last time a person here was killed by a polar bear was nearly twenty years ago. The bear was after some meat that the man was carrying.'

'What happened to the bear?' Mandy dreaded the answer, but she appreciated the way in which Alicia had tried to explain the bear's actions.

'It had to be killed,' Alicia said sadly. 'That's

why it's so important to keep the bears out on the tundra where they belong and not encourage them into the town. That's the job my dad has, though at times it's quite difficult! Like now, when they're really hungry. They can smell food in the town, and the dump especially draws them like a magnet! My dad works closely with the research station,' Alicia added, 'so he knows a lot about the bears. I want to have a job just like his when I finish school.'

'I'm going to be a vet,' Mandy said. 'Like my mum and dad.' She started to tell Alicia all about Animal Ark, and the domestic and wild animals which her parents treated in surgery.

'Your home sounds great,' said Alicia. 'Sometimes I'd like a break from the cold, maybe I'll come and visit you one day. By the way, you'll be here for Hallowe'en, won't you?'

'Yes, I think so,' Mandy replied.

'Would you like to come trick-or-treating with me?'

'I'd love to!' Mandy exclaimed. 'Will I need a costume?'

'Don't worry, we've got a box of things we can dress up in, or my mom can run you up something on her sewing machine,' Alicia said confidently.

'Alicia?' John Bruce hollered from the bottom of the stairs. 'You up there?'

'Yes!' Alicia called back.

'Come down for a moment, will you?' her father shouted. 'I'm making plans with the Hopes for a sky ride tomorrow morning.'

'Oh, great!' cried Alicia, wriggling off the bed. 'You'll love that, Mandy!'

'Sky ride?' asked Mandy, hurrying after Alicia who had shot out of the door. 'What's that?'

'Dad uses a helicopter for his job to find the bears out on the tundra that need to be tagged or given treatment,' Alicia explained over her shoulder. 'It's the best way of seeing the bears. You can fly way out over Cape Churchill, where they're beginning to gather because that's where the bay freezes first.'

'That sounds amazing!' Mandy beamed. 'Does it frighten them? The noise of the helicopter, I mean.' She clattered down the stairs after Alicia. Mandy had seen films of light aircraft flying low over the African plains, scattering whole herds of terrified zebra or antelope below.

'Some bears don't seem to care, but others will

run away,' Alicia answered. 'They get used to things very quickly. After all, they don't mind the tundra buggies any more.'

That was true, Mandy reflected. She had seen how calm the bears were around the big vehicle. And it would be great to get a bird's eye view of this amazing land.

'Can I go with Mandy?' Alicia asked her father, the moment she arrived in the kitchen.

'Well now, it's only a four-seater, sweetheart,' her father reminded her. 'Adam and Emily will be on board too. You can come along any time and, besides, Hamish has just started his new medication, so you should probably keep an eye on him for a couple of days.'

Alicia looked around for the little dog. He was curled in a small wicker basket on a tartan rug. He looked up at her and cocked his head, his bright, brown eyes loyal and loving.

'That's a good point, Dad,' Alicia said at once, stooping to pet him.

'What's wrong with him?' Mandy asked. She looked carefully at Hamish to see what she could have missed.

'Most of the time, he's fit as a fiddle,' John

Bruce chimed in. 'But the wee chap has epilepsy.'

'I have to give Hamish a tablet at the same time every day,' Alicia explained.

'Oh, poor Hamish,' Mandy said. She had once seen a dog having a fit on the operating table at Animal Ark. She remembered her mother holding on to the dog's tongue to stop it from biting it by accident.

'Shall I stay behind with you?' Mandy offered.

Her friend grinned. 'No, don't worry about me – or Hamish. We're used to it by now. You go and have a great time. You could take some more photos for me!'

'OK.' Mandy looked up at Alicia's father. 'Thanks, Mr Bruce!'

'Let's join your mum and dad, then,' he said. 'They're buried under a mountain of journals in my office! Come on.'

While the Hopes were looking at a map to see where they would be flying the following morning, Mrs Bruce arrived home. She put her head around the door of the office, smiling in welcome. Alicia, Mandy noticed, looked exactly like her mother – the same fine dark hair and almond-shaped eyes.

When the introductions were over, Grace Bruce insisted they all stayed for dinner. 'I haven't had a chance to get to know you all, the way John has!' she exclaimed, when Emily Hope politely protested. 'You must stay.'

During the meal, the talk was mainly of polar bears. Mr Bruce entertained them with stories about his work with the 'white giants', as he affectionately called them. He also told them more about the sky ride, explaining that the helicopters were part of a special bear patrol team that was on duty twenty-four hours a day.

'My loyalties are divided between four-legged and two-legged animals,' Mr Bruce said, winking at Mandy. 'I have to protect the local people from the bears, who can get pretty mean and hungry at this time of year, but I'm also responsible for the bears' welfare while they're migrating through Churchill.'

As he talked, Mandy realised how important Mr Bruce's work was to him. And to Alicia, she added silently, noticing that her friend's eyes shone with enthusiasm as she listened to her father.

It was well past eleven when they gathered up their coats to leave. Mandy shivered in anticipation of the cold walk back to their hotel.

'What a lovely family!' Emily Hope remarked, as they set off along the pavement.

'You and Alicia seemed to get on well,' said Mandy's dad.

'She's really nice,' Mandy replied. She yawned and looked up at the velvet dark sky, aglow with a million stars. 'Oh, what's that?' she gasped, pointing.

A vast, flickering display of coloured lights blazed on the horizon. Clouds of red, green and white smudged the sky, hanging in an arc against the midnight blue of the Arctic night.

'It's the aurora borealis!' Mr Hope answered. 'What a stunning sight! Those colours are caused by tiny electron particles bouncing around in the atmosphere.'

'It's better than a firework display!' Mandy exclaimed, craning her neck to watch in awe the spectacular light-show. Now, a soft green glow painted the sky, filled with sparkling, shooting colours.

'Nature's firework display,' Emily Hope

breathed beside her. 'Isn't it fantastic?'

Mandy smiled. Her mum was right. It *was* fantastic, like just about everything in this extraordinary land. And now she had a helicopter ride to look forward to as well, with the chance to see even more polar bears.

Three

Adam Hope steered their rented four-wheel drive vehicle into a parking space at the edge of the airstrip, keeping a careful distance from the gently rotating blade of the helicopter. Ice chips blowing in from the tundra dusted the three other helicopters standing on the tarmac.

Mandy pulled on her mittens and waved as Alicia came over. She was holding Hamish, who was wearing a warm red jacket. Emily and Adam Hope greeted Mr Bruce, who was just behind Alicia, and followed him across the tarmac to the helicopter.

'Great weather for a flight!' Alicia said to Mandy, glancing up at the cloudless sky. 'You should have a good view of the bears.'

'Are you coming?" Mandy asked her hopefully. She hadn't expected to see Alicia this morning.

'No, Hamish and I will wait in the airstrip office over there,' Alicia smiled. 'I've just come to see you off.'

Mandy walked over to the helicopter and climbed in. Her mum and dad grinned at her as they fastened their seatbelts. Once she had strapped herself into her seat at the back of the helicopter, Mandy peered around uncertainly at the glass bubble surrounding her. It didn't seem very sturdy. She tapped lightly on the glass, testing its strength, and caught sight of Alicia grinning at her from the door of the airstrip office.

'You'll be fine!' Alicia mouthed, as the engine sprang to life. The blades whipped up a powerful wind. The hood of her coat had fallen back and her hair rose in a cloud around her head. She waved cheerily as the helicopter lifted off the ground.

'Bye, Alicia!' Mandy called.

'See you, lass!' Mr Bruce shouted to his daughter

as he piloted the helicopter into the sky.

'Just look at the amazing scenery!' Adam Hope remarked, as they swooped away from the town and headed over the endless tundra. 'It's an ice desert.'

Mandy gazed down at the land below. There were no colours to see, none at all. Just white, as though the land had been iced, like a giant cake.

'It looks deep, but the ice over the bay won't be solid enough for the polar bears to go out hunting for a few weeks yet,' said Mr Bruce.

'Good!' Mandy said to her mother, who was sitting beside her in the back. 'That means we'll get to see lots more bears.'

'Look down there,' Mr Bruce said urgently, pointing to the right. 'Red fox. See it?'

'Oh, where?' Mandy peered through the glass window, and spotted the animal. It streaked across the ice in a blur of dark red fur.

The helicopter flew on towards the shore of Hudson Bay. When Mandy next looked down, she saw what she thought at first were lumpy deposits of ice. But then she spotted the coal-black buttons

of the bears' noses and gave a shriek. 'Polars!
Look, Mum!'

There was a small group of bears directly below.
John Bruce flew towards them, changing course
and descending quite suddenly. Mandy's heart
began to pound with excitement, and she felt a
lurching sensation in her stomach as they
dropped downwards.

Adam Hope fumbled with his camera. 'This is
going to be terrific!' he shouted enthusiastically.

The hovering helicopter cast a flickering
shadow on the ice. The bears looked up. A few of
them began to scatter, running from the throb of
the approaching engine. One small bear seemed
determined to put as much distance between him
and the helicopter as he could. The others
continued to play or feed, clawing at the clumps
of ice-covered kelp that grew along the shoreline.

John Bruce immediately altered their course
again, turning the helicopter so that they headed
up and away from the group.

'Oh, why are we leaving?' Mandy asked,
disappointed. Her forehead was pressed against
the glass as she tried to keep the small galloping
bear in sight.

'I must be careful not to alarm them, Mandy,' Mr Bruce explained. 'At this time of year, the bears can't afford the energy it takes for them to run because they must save it for when they go out on to the ice. Also, they are so well insulated against the cold that if they get too warm they can become exhausted – and even die.'

'Oh!' Mandy twisted in her seat to look back at the bears. The ones that had broken from the group had stopped. They looked up at the sky suspiciously.

'We're getting a good enough view from where we are—' Mrs Hope began, but her sentence was cut short. John Bruce's radio had crackled to life. There were several seconds of hissing, then a man's voice came through. He spoke urgently, barking out a code of some kind. Mandy leaned forward in her seat so she could hear.

'I read you, Mike,' Mr Bruce said, speaking loudly into the mouthpiece attached to his earphones.

'A female and two cubs . . . running in Churchill . . . Can you help?' said the voice on the radio.

'Can do. I'm on my way back now, Mike,' John Bruce replied, steering the helicopter in a broad arc to the west. 'Where are they headed?'

'The dump.' Mike sounded tense. 'Try and head them off, will you? We've got a coachload of tourists just arrived in town.'

'No problem. I'm on my way. Over and out.' John Bruce turned to the Hopes and shrugged apologetically. 'Sorry about this. Duty calls.'

'What's happened?' asked Mandy, who wasn't certain she'd followed the conversation.

'A group of bears has come into town in search of something to eat. All the helicopters will be mobilised to try and head them off,' Mr Bruce explained.

'Are you going to land? I mean, drop us off?' Mandy asked, hoping he wasn't.

'There's no time for that.' Mr Bruce shook his head. 'We need to try and chase this particular group back on to the tundra as soon as possible.'

Mandy felt a thrill of excitement. She was going to be involved in a real-life polar bear mission! She turned to her mother and lowered her voice. 'They won't be hurt, will they?'

Emily Hope shook her head. 'These bears are

protected, love. The men are trying to help them, that's all.'

'We take great care of our polar bears, Mandy,' Mr Bruce assured her. 'Our aim is to discourage them from raiding the town for food and using the locals for lunch!'

Mandy grinned and looked down to see if she could spot the bears. The streets of the town were spread out below them. A group of small

children were playing a game, jumping in and out of a complicated pattern which they had drawn in an unspoiled stretch of snow. Along the main street, the heavy tyre tracks of four-wheel drive vehicles, and the ski marks of sleighs and snowmobiles, had carved up the smooth frosting of ice.

John Bruce tapped on the glass of the windscreen. 'Judging by the crowd that's gathered over there, my guess is we've located our bears,' he said.

'And here comes the cavalry!' Mr Hope added cheerfully.

Two more helicopters had appeared in the sky. They hovered low over the tops of the wooden houses, whipping up a froth of snow with their whirring blades. As Mandy watched, a third helicopter rose up from behind a tall concrete building. The throb of the four powerful engines was deafening.

'I can't get in any closer.' John Bruce spoke loudly. 'And there's no sign of the bears.'

Down on the ground, Mandy could see a man in a uniform ushering people off the street. They were being herded into shops and houses, and the doors closed firmly behind them.

Suddenly, Mandy spotted a blurry movement out of the corner of her eye. 'There!' she yelled. 'I can see a *cub*!'

'You're right, Mandy,' Mr Bruce agreed. 'There's a little fellow, all right. The mother bear shouldn't be far behind.'

The small white cub was running along a narrow street. Confused and frightened, it approached a parked truck and squeezed underneath it. Within seconds the mother bear broke from the cover of an open doorway. A second cub was hard on her heels.

Mandy's heart turned over. 'There!' she shouted. 'All three of them. What's going to happen now?'

'We're going to try and head them out of town,' Mr Bruce said. He spoke into his headset, making contact with the other pilots. The babble of radio voices faded to the background as Mandy concentrated fiercely on keeping the three bears in sight.

The smaller of the cubs backed out from under the truck, summoned by the urgent bark of his mother. She led them in a lumbering run along the road. The four helicopters hovered overhead.

The little cub stopped to look up a side street and Mandy saw the mother bear grab it by the scruff of its neck with her teeth, giving it a swift shaking. Then she set him roughly down and took the lead, glancing round to make sure both cubs were following.

'Are they heading out of town?' Adam Hope asked, raising his voice above the noise of the helicopter.

'Nope.' Mr Bruce shook his head in frustration. 'They're still making for the dump!'

'Obviously, the thought of food is more tempting than getting away from the noise we're making,' Mrs Hope shouted from the back.

'Yep, this lot are determined all right!' John Bruce was frowning hard. He spoke into his headset again. 'It's not working, Bill . . .' Mandy heard him say. 'She's taking them into the dump.'

Mandy held on to her seat as John Bruce tipped the nose of the helicopter as low as he dared. Mandy thought that the mother bear looked thin and ravenous, and she was obviously determined to reach her destination. She held her course, ignoring the helicopters buzzing overhead as she made for the mountain of black plastic bags.

'We're going to have to give chase on foot,' Mr Bruce told his passengers. 'And that means landing the helicopters back at base, and loading up with all the gear.'

'Tranquillising darts?' Adam Hope guessed.

'That's right, Adam.' John Bruce nodded and turned to look at Emily Hope and Mandy. 'Well, I bet you didn't expect to see all this today!'

'It's an experience for us,' Mrs Hope replied. 'We certainly don't get this in Welford!'

Mr Bruce winked at Mandy over his shoulder. 'Are you bearing up, lass?'

'It's so exciting!' Mandy exclaimed, her eyes wide.

'Right, let's get back then,' John Bruce announced. 'We'll start tracking on foot!'

Four

Mandy unclipped her seatbelt as soon as the helicopter touched down. During the short flight back to base, her concern for the welfare of the mother bear and her cubs had grown. What if, crazed by hunger, the bear attacked someone in the town and was shot? Her twins would not survive without their mother. Mandy hoped that John Bruce would be able to get the bears safely back on to the tundra before anything bad happened.

The John Bruce's helicopter had flown in formation with the three other pilots who had

joined them in the attempt to steer the bears out
of the town. Now the men scrambled from their
cockpits and rushed to get ready. Mr and Mrs
Hope lent a hand in sorting out the equipment
for the chase. Powerful flashlights and
tranquillising dart guns were being loaded into
bright yellow four-wheel drive vehicles which were
parked in front of the airstrip office.

As Mandy walked across the tarmac, she saw
Alicia hurrying towards her. Hamish's jet black
nose and his bristly whiskers peeped over the top
of her parka.

'I heard from Dad there are polar bears in
town!' Alicia said breathlessly.

'Yes, a mum and twin cubs,' Mandy confirmed.
'I hope they'll be OK.'

'Don't worry.' Alicia smiled encouragingly at
her. 'Dad'll help them get out of the town. Nobody
knows polar bears the way he does – he's the best.'

'Come on, Mandy!' Mr Hope yelled from the
driver's seat of their rented four-wheel drive.
'We're going to stick with John, in case we're
needed.'

Mandy ran over to the car and jumped in, while
Alicia joined her dad in his distinctive bear patrol

Land-rover. Adam Hope revved the engine of his Jeep and joined the line of vehicles heading out of the gate and back into Churchill.

'These polar bears are a full-time job!' said Emily Hope, using her fingers to untangle the knotted ends of her long red hair.

'But only for a small part of the year,' Mr Hope reminded her. 'Once the bay's frozen, they'll be gone for another year.'

In the back, Mandy eased her cold fingers out of her gloves and waved to Alicia in the Land-rover ahead of them. John Bruce was driving as fast as he could on the icy road, and Mandy could see by her dad's frown of concentration that he was finding it difficult to keep up.

'Keep going, Dad,' Mandy urged, her excitement mounting. 'We've got to get those bears back on to the tundra!'

'Well, they've had a head start on us,' Mrs Hope remarked. 'They did seem determined, I must say.'

'John's pulling up,' said Adam Hope, steering into the side of the road. 'This must be the dump.'

Mandy looked out. Through a wire mesh fence, she could see an acre or so of land which had been scorched a sooty black by the burning of waste. A row of yellow bulldozers loomed like metallic giants at the far side of the area, their engines silent. Towering stacks of bulging black bin-liners were piled against the tall wire fence. Here and there the plastic had been ripped open, and their contents trailed in the dirt.

Car doors slammed all around them as the sheriff's team jumped out of their vehicles.

John Bruce cupped his hand round the butt of the dart gun, the long muzzle resting against his shoulder. 'Quiet now,' he ordered. 'We don't want to worry them.' He and the other men looked around intently.

Mandy made her way to where Alicia stood cradling Hamish, who snoozed in the pouch of her thick parka. Alicia unzipped the jacket and the little dog peeped out at Mandy, blinking in the light.

'Hi, Hamish,' Mandy whispered.

'Hush!' John Bruce commanded. Mandy felt her face flush hot.

In the silence, the distinct sound of lapping could be heard coming from behind a tall stack of black sacks. Mr Bruce motioned for the team to spread out around the stack. Stepping lightly, the men followed Mr Bruce's instructions.

Mandy's heart began to beat hard. Where *were* the cubs? She strained to see.

Silently, John Bruce led the team towards the sound of slurping and sucking.

'Sounds as though the mother bear has found something to eat,' Emily Hope whispered to Mandy.

Mandy watched Mr Bruce as he picked his way through the scattered litter. Then, suddenly, she saw him stumble and fall heavily to his side. The bottle he'd tripped over spun away from under him and struck the side of the fence with a loud clang.

The big polar bear reared up on her hindlegs from behind the rubbish sacks, just a few metres from the wire fence. She was over two metres tall. Mandy gasped as the bear began to make a loud huffing sound, snapping her jaws and lowering her head. She dropped heavily on to all fours and broke into a trot, heading straight for the gate of the dump – and for John Bruce, who lay directly in the path of the fleeing bear.

The cubs scuttled after her. Mandy looked across at Alicia – her hand covered her mouth and her eyes were wide with alarm. She clearly

knew she couldn't call out to her father, who lay still, covering his head with both hands, while the men aimed their tranquillising guns at the adult bear's lolloping back. One of them fired, and missed. Mandy's heart lurched in her chest as she saw the man carrying a shotgun take aim. He had to be ready to fire, in case the big female bear decided to attack the polar sheriff.

But the bear gathered speed and galloped past John Bruce as he lay face down on the ground. She made it through the gate and on to the road, her padded paws pounding into the tarmac, reaching a speed Mandy hadn't thought big bears could achieve.

The man with the shotgun trained on the polar bear's back lowered it. 'You OK, John?' he shouted to Mr Bruce.

'I'm fine,' he called, scrambling to his feet and brushing at the dirt he'd picked up on the front of his jacket. 'We'll have to go after her. She's a wily one, I'll say that!' He ran to the gate of the dump and looked after the polar bear. Her pace had slowed to a brisk trot and she was making her way steadily up the street with her cubs beside her.

Just then, Mandy heard Alicia shout. She turned to see Hamish writhing round frantically inside Alicia's coat. He scrabbled to be free, tearing at the fabric of her coat with his claws. And then he bounded to the ground and streaked up the road after the bear.

'Hamish!' Alicia wailed. 'You silly dog! Come back!'

Mandy stared after the little dog in dismay. She dashed to Alicia's side.

'He's going after the bear!' Alicia exclaimed. Then she called out to her father. 'Dad! Hamish has run away!' She looked pale and anxious. 'I've got to get him back, Mandy,' she pleaded.

'Surely Hamish wouldn't try and tackle a polar bear?' Mandy said, trying to reassure Alicia a little.

'Who knows what he will do?' Alicia zipped up her torn parka jacket. 'But I don't want him to get close enough to even try! Besides, it's almost time for his medicine.'

'We'll find him,' Mandy said confidently, though she was rather alarmed at the thought of charging after a dog that had run in the direction of an angry, starving bear. 'Shall I follow him?'

'Hold on, lass,' Mr Bruce said softly, coming

up to them. He was limping slightly. He put a hand on Alicia's shoulder. 'We've got to go after the mother bear,' he said. 'There's not a moment to waste. You and Mandy can follow behind us, but keep your distance, and stop at once if I say so.'

'OK, Dad,' said Alicia.

'Over here!' Mr Bruce called, beckoning to the others.

The team of four men gathered around him.

'Let's split up,' he went on. 'Bill and Mike, you take Main Street West. Dave and Wayne stay here, in case she doubles back to the dump. If you see her, don't dart her unless you're sure of a clean hit. We don't want to antagonise her. We'll start with the tracks at the gate.'

'I'm going after Hamish,' Alicia said, setting out in the direction the dog had run.

'You stick with me!' John Bruce ordered. 'We'll go east with Adam and Emily, and Mandy. Adam, will you carry this pack?'

'Sure.' Mr Hope took the blue canvas backpack and slipped it on to his shoulders.

'Right. Let's go, then. Everyone keep a sharp look out for prints on the ground. OK?'

The serious-faced party set out along the street. John Bruce walked ahead, following the impressions left by the bear in the snow. Mandy's mum and dad were directly behind him, with Alicia and Mandy bringing up the rear. Nobody spoke, but Emily Hope turned and smiled encouragingly at Mandy.

Mandy noticed that it had begun to snow. The sky had turned a muddy shade of yellow, and tiny flakes floated down around them. Mandy felt frustrated that the polar bear family had escaped John Bruce's team. If they had been successfully rounded up, they would be on their way back to the tundra, out of harm's way. And now there was Hamish to worry about, too.

'We'd better hurry,' she urged Alicia. 'We don't want Hamish's pawprints to be covered by fresh snow.'

'There they go.' Alicia pointed to the tiny canine pawprints. 'And there – and here, he's turned right!'

'Hamish!' Mandy called.

'Here, Hamish!' shouted Alicia.

Then Mandy spotted a second set of prints in the snow. These were much larger and, in the tell-tale way of bears, were pigeon-toed. 'The bear has been this way too!' she gasped, grabbing Alicia's sleeve.

It was out before Mandy could stop herself, and Alicia looked even paler. 'Hamish! Hamish!' she called again.

'Easy, lass,' said her father, coming up the side street behind them. 'Go quietly. We'll find the wee dog.' He walked past them, peering at the ground through the rapidly falling snowflakes.

The narrow street appeared to be deserted. From time to time as they trudged along, Mandy glimpsed a face looking out from a curtained window. Her fingers began to ache with cold inside her gloves. She had long ago lost any feeling in her freezing toes.

'Hamish!' Alicia called, a desperate note in her voice. Mandy wished she could comfort her friend but there was nothing she could do except hope that Hamish had found a sensible hiding place.

Ahead of them, John Bruce broke into a run. He held the tranquillising gun with both hands, close to his chest.

It was becoming difficult to see as the snow

thickened and filled in the tracks on the ground. Mandy was just beginning to think she could not go on much farther when they rounded a corner – and came face to face with the polar bear.

She was weary of the chase, Mandy could tell, and was slumped against the wall of a wooden shed. The cubs were pressed as close to her side as they could get.

'There now.' John Bruce stopped, breathing hard. He slowly moved his hand along the gun and flicked the safety catch. 'There you are, my beauty.'

Mandy heard her mum and dad come to a halt just behind her.

'Oh, Hamish!' Alicia whispered. 'Please be safe!' But there was no sign of the little black dog.

Mandy's legs turned to jelly. She felt as if her heart was going to burst through her ribcage. She was thrilled to be this close to the polar bear, but she knew that the mother would be feeling very frustrated and desperate to protect her cubs. Mandy looked around for somewhere to hide.

Alicia reached out very slowly and took Mandy's hand. Gently, they backed away, each step seeming to take an age. Mandy tried to stop her teeth from chattering. It sounded so loud in the snow-filled silence.

The polar bear stood on her hindlegs. Her head swayed from side to side and she showed her teeth in a low grumbling growl. Mandy could feel the hairs on the back of her neck stand on end. She was amazed at how brave Alicia's father was. The huge bear stared directly at him, perfectly balanced on her back legs, but John Bruce didn't move a muscle. He slowly raised the tranquillising gun to his shoulder and peered along the barrel, aiming for the bear's chest. He looked up again, and Mandy wondered if he was finding it difficult to see through the thickly swirling snow.

Suddenly, one of the cubs decided to run for it. It broke away from its mother and scampered round the side of the building. In the silent, nerve-wracking seconds that followed, it seemed to Mandy that the mother bear was trying to weigh up whether to go after it, or stay and confront the humans threatening the remaining cub.

But she didn't get a chance to decide. Mr Bruce found his mark through the falling snow – and fired.

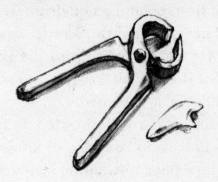

Five

The polar bear jumped as the dart penetrated the big muscle of her right shoulder. She looked down at it, before she began to stagger. Her massive front paws hit the ground with a thud and she rolled her eyes, baring her teeth.

Mandy clutched at Alicia. How long would the dart take to work?

'I hope the drug works quickly,' Alicia whispered, as if in answer to Mandy's thoughts. 'This is when they're at their most dangerous.'

All was quiet for a moment, except for the soft, menacing growl of the bear. Suddenly, Hamish leaped out from behind an oil-drum wedged into the ice. The foolish little Scottie was yapping furiously. He ran straight up to the polar bear, snarling, his stumpy tail wagging in excitement.

'Hamish!' Alicia screamed.

'Stay back, you two!' shouted John Bruce. 'Hamish will have to take care of himself.'

Adam Hope put a restraining hand on Mandy's arm. Then he raised his tranquilliser gun to cover the polar sheriff, just in case.

Mandy saw that Mr Bruce's dart gun was also raised again. He was ready to fire a second shot. Her heart thudded in her chest, and her whole body seemed to have frozen in fear. Beside her, Alicia gasped as Hamish bounded round the bewildered bear, growling his fiercest growl and trying to nip at her feet. The polar bear tried to follow the dog with her head, but her movements were becoming slow and heavy. Mandy saw her eyelids begin to droop, as the drug took effect, and the massive bear rolled gracefully on to her side. A great sigh escaped her as her head flopped on to her front paws.

'Don't anybody move,' Mr Bruce warned them. 'She may not be fully under yet.'

Mandy reminded herself to breathe. Her eyes were fixed on the little cub, who was trying to bury himself between his mother's furry front legs. He paddled his paws in the snow as he burrowed, nosing at her and squealing faintly. It made Mandy want to rush forward and gather him up into her arms.

'Oh, poor little thing,' she whispered.

'Is she asleep yet?' Alicia asked her father. On the far side of the bear, Hamish stood stiff-legged, his hackles raised. He kept up an angry snarling, sniffing furiously at the slumped bear.

'I'll find out in a minute,' Mr Bruce answered. He took a step towards the felled bear. With a squeak, the terrified cub cuddled closer to its mother. Cautiously, John Bruce approached, then he put out his boot and pushed it against the bear's chest. She grunted, and her head lolled.

'She's out,' Mr Bruce announced cheerfully, clicking the safety-catch on his tranquillising gun. 'Now, I'll have to give the cub a small dose of the drug by hand. He's too wee for a dart the size his mother got.' He looked round at Mr Hope. 'Adam, could get you a syringe out of the pack?'

As soon as her father declared the bear was out

cold, Alicia ran towards Hamish. In a second, she had scooped him up into her arms and was covering his head with kisses. 'Silly, silly dog!' she chided, clutching him to her chest. 'Oh, Hamish, you could have been that bear's lunch!'

Mandy stroked Hamish's velvety ears. They were freezing to the touch. The little dog was shivering all over with cold and excitement. Mandy was relieved he was safely back with Alicia, but she couldn't help feeling very worried about the cubs. One had disappeared, and the other was clearly in distress. Mandy went to stand beside her mum. There was ice on Emily Hope's eyelashes and her nose was bright red with the cold.

John Bruce squatted down by the head of the mother bear. Mandy saw the little cub peep out at the looming human. The end of his small black nose was just visible between his mother's front paws, which had crossed over when she'd fallen on her side. The cub ducked down, trying to use his mother's furry embrace as a hiding place, but then, as John Bruce reached out with one hand, he seemed to think better of the idea. He eased his little body out backwards, looking around him nervously, and made a dash for freedom.

'Grab him!' John Bruce shouted to Adam Hope, as the cub made straight towards him. Mr Hope lunged for the little bear, blocking its path with arms spread wide. The cub wheeled about, and Mr Bruce wrestled it to the ground. 'Got you!' he said.

'Have you got that syringe, Adam?' Mr Bruce held the struggling cub firmly on the ground.

Adam Hope took the syringe from his backpack and inserted it quickly into the cub's neck. Within a few seconds, his little bear went limp in Mr Bruce's grasp. He was deeply asleep.

'Phew!' said John Bruce. 'He's stronger than he looks!' He unclipped the radio from his belt and spoke urgently into it, telling the other members of the team where to find him.

'Are they all right?' Mandy asked, looking down at the sleeping bears.

'Sure, they're fine,' Mr Bruce replied. 'They're just unconscious. They'll stay like that for the next two or three hours.' Mr Bruce lifted the female bear's small ears and peered inside, first one, then the other.

'No tag? No tattoo?' Adam Hope asked. He and Emily Hope kneeled in the snow, closely examining the bear and her cub.

'No, we've not caught her before,' John Bruce said.

'What will happen to the other cub?' Mandy asked anxiously.

'Don't worry,' replied Mr Bruce, smiling at her. 'I'll send a team out for him as soon as we get this pair loaded on to the truck. He won't have got far.'

Just then, a bright yellow Land-rover drew up behind them, carrying the rest of John Bruce's team. The men quickly arranged the sleeping bear's heavy body so that she could breathe comfortably; all four of her legs were stretched out straight in front of her, and her head was tipped downwards so that she would pick up the comforting scent of her cub lying close to her chest.

'This cub's a female,' Adam Hope told them. 'She can't be much more than seven months old, which is why she's smaller than the other cubs you see at this time of year.'

'She's gorgeous!' Mandy said. She put out a hand to the drowsy cub and stroked it. The fur was thick and rough and very dirty, but Mandy was thrilled to be able to make contact with a real, live polar bear. She soothed it with the flat of her hand, hoping that, as it slept, the cub would find some comfort in her touch.

'She's pretty lean,' one of John Bruce's men commented. He felt the mother bear's body with his hands. 'I can feel the whole of her pelvis. Poor girl – it's hard work keeping up enough body fat for herself as well as the cubs.'

Emily Hope stood up and took Mandy's hands in her own. She rubbed them gently. 'How long will she go on feeding her twins?' she asked the polar team member.

'Another year or so,' he told her. 'She'll be fine once she gets out on to the ice, but she's as thin as any bear I've seen so far this year.'

The bear grumbled in her sleep and her eyelids trembled. Mr Bruce attached a metal tag to her ear, which carried an identification number. Next, he deftly extracted a tooth with a small pair of pliers he took from Adam Hope's backpack.

The size of the tooth surprised Mandy. 'It's as big as a wedge of lemon!' she exclaimed.

'This tooth will tell us a lot about the bear, besides her age,' he said, dropping it into a plastic bag. 'We can analyse it to see if she's getting the right vitamins and minerals in her diet. If she's been even more short of food than usual, her teeth won't have developed properly.'

'Dad?' Alicia spoke up. 'I want to take Hamish home. He's freezing.'

'Will you ask someone to drive you, lass?' her father said. 'I need to get these two to the polar bear jail before they wake up. And I need to sort out a search team for the missing cub.'

'I'll take you,' a man offered. 'Then I'll go in search of the cub, if you like.'

'Thanks, Bill,' said Mr Bruce. 'Take Dale with you, and radio in to let me know if you find him. There's not much time before it'll be too dark for a thorough look.' Mr Bruce glanced at his wrist-watch. It was only three o'clock, but Mandy noticed that the daylight was already fading.

Alicia carried Hamish to the yellow Land-rover. 'Bye, everyone,' she said, opening the door and putting the little dog on the passenger seat.

'Bye, Alicia. I hope Hamish will be OK,' Mandy called. Then she turned to her father. 'What did Mr Bruce mean about taking the polar bears to jail, Dad? Does he mean like a prison?'

'No, it's not a prison, Mandy.' Adam Hope laughed. 'It's more like a safe place where the bears can be held until the bay freezes.'

'Can people visit them there?' Mandy asked.

Her dad shook his head. 'I shouldn't think so. It isn't a tourist attraction. The bears aren't even fed there as it would encourage them to come back to the town again,' he explained. 'They just get given water, which they would find outside anyway.'

As the mid-afternoon twilight approached, lights began to shine cosily from the windows of the houses in the town. Mandy thought again of the tiny cub, wandering around on its own in search of its mother. It was going to be even harder to find the little cub in the dark, but Mandy was keen to keep looking, in spite of the bitter cold.

'John, can we do anything to help find the missing cub?' Adam Hope asked.

'Good of you to offer,' said Mr Bruce. 'But it would be better if you could help me to get the pair we've got here to the jail.' As he spoke, he was measuring the circumference of the polar bear's head, and her length and breadth, with a plastic tape measure. He scribbled each measurement in a small notebook. 'We have to make these two our priority, then we'll help Bill and Dale track down the missing cub, if there's still any daylight.' He looked up. 'Oh, good, here comes Mike with the flat-bed.'

One of John Bruce's men was backing a large open-backed truck down the narrow street. He jumped out, and helped Mr Bruce and Mandy's dad to drag the massive body of the mother polar bear on to a canvas stretcher, then heave her up into the open back of the truck. Between them, Adam Hope and Mr Bruce picked up the cub and placed it gently beside her. Its small face was swallowed up in the shaggy fur of its mother's giant front leg.

'There,' John Bruce said with satisfaction. 'All set for the journey, Mike.' He turned to Mandy and her parents. 'Fancy a trip to the polar jail?' he offered with a grin. 'It's one of the most interesting parts of the polar experience!'

For a moment Mandy thought her mother might refuse, and Mandy wouldn't have blamed her. It was so cold she ached, and the thought of Alicia's cosy little bedroom and a steaming mug of hot chocolate was very tempting. But Mandy knew this was an experience not to be missed. 'Count me in,' Mandy said.

Emily Hope smiled. 'Yes, we'll all come along,' she said.

'Right you are,' said Mr Bruce, as he hastily stuffed his equipment into the backpack. 'There's not a moment to lose.' He nodded in the direction of the vehicle. 'As you can see . . .'

With a start, Mandy realised that the big female

had opened one of her eyes. She was trying to raise her head from her paws.

'Everybody get in the truck' Mr Bruce ordered. 'Mike, I'll drive. You ride on the back.' He tossed the tranquilliser gun across to his colleague, who caught it deftly. 'Quick now! Let's go.'

Six

Mandy rode in the front of the truck next to John Bruce. Her mum and dad sat in a row of seats just behind them. In the back of the truck, the mother polar bear lay with her head lolling on her paws. Mandy thought she looked very peaceful, jogging along with her cub tucked in beside her. Mike crouched beside them, one hand clinging to the side of the truck and the other cradling the tranquilliser gun. Mandy hoped they would reach the polar jail before he needed to use it again.

She turned to John Bruce. 'If the bears keep

coming to the dump,' she asked, 'why don't you just fence it off to stop them?'

'That's not possible, Mandy,' Mr Bruce replied, offering Mandy a biscuit from a packet stowed in the glove compartment. She took one gratefully. 'Male bears weigh as much as seventeen hundred pounds – they can tear down fences as easy as cracking a nut. Also, the gates would have to be kept open, to allow the garbage trucks in.'

'Then why don't the bears go further north?' Mandy persisted. 'There must be seals they could hunt up there?'

'That's a good question.' John Bruce looked sideways at her briefly and grinned. 'But there are bears up there already. A polar bear that goes into unknown territory is asking for trouble. Male bears can be extremely aggressive. Besides, these bears have grown up around here. Churchill is the place they know. The problem is, as the bears get hungrier, they're prepared to come into town more often.'

'Can't you feed them?' Mandy suggested. 'I mean, like they do in a zoo?'

'In no time at all we'd have hundreds of bears prowling around Churchill waiting for food,' Mr

Bruce explained. 'That wouldn't please the locals, I can tell you!'

'Don't they like the bears?' asked Mandy.

'It's not that they don't like them,' Mr Bruce said. 'But they want to feel safe. That's why they rely on us to do our job efficiently, especially at this time of the year. The polar bears attract thousands of tourists to Churchill every year, and the local people appreciate that – tourism means money for their businesses.'

Mandy nodded, looking thoughtful. The fluffy toy polar bears she had seen in the shop windows were proof of how important the bears were as a tourist attraction.

John Bruce turned right off the main road and brought the truck to a gentle stop outside a huge metal building. 'Welcome to the polar jail,' he said, switching off the ignition and climbing out of the cab. Mandy slithered across the seat and followed him.

Wide and windowless, the jail looked more like a warehouse than anything else. Mandy spotted a strange-looking object parked outside. It was a large drum, lying on its side, on wheels. There was an iron grille bolted across the front.

'What's that?' she asked, walking over to have a closer look.

'It's a bear trap,' Mr Bruce explained. 'It's one of about fifteen we use at this time of the year. We hang a piece of meat in it and try to catch the bears before they make it into the town in search of food.'

Just then, a shout from Mike in the back of the truck made them look round. Mandy's mum and dad had climbed out of the cab, and Adam Hope was standing on the wheel arch of the truck, looking in on the polar bear.

'She's trying to get to her feet,' he called out. 'Not very successfully,' he added.

'Right,' said John Bruce, 'we'll have to move quickly.'

Mandy helped her father unlock the trailer flap. The polar bear's eyes were wide open now, but she lay quite still, blinking. Suddenly, her whole body began to shudder.

'What's wrong with her?' Mandy whispered, alarmed.

'She's having a small convulsion,' Adam Hope explained calmly. 'She's under a lot of stress. Knowing we're here her first instinct is to attack us, but she can't move. Don't worry, she'll be fine.'

Mike jumped off the back of the truck and went to unlock the polar jail. With a resounding clang, the big metal door swung open to reveal two rows of caged rooms.

John Bruce sprang into the truck and crouched down by the head of the polar bear, lifting her lips to reveal her gums. 'Still a nice, healthy pink. That's good,' he announced. 'If they were very pale, it would mean that she'd gone into shock and her circulation had slowed right down. Adam, help me to lift her on to the stretcher, will you? Then we can get her down to the ground. Emily, Mandy, can you get the cub out first?'

Mandy was pleased to be able to help. She put her hands under the arms of the little bear's front legs and lifted. She was lighter than Mandy expected. Her head lolled sleepily against Mandy's shoulder, as Emily Hope carefully lifted her back legs.

They carried the little cub across the snow-covered concrete and into the building. Everywhere Mandy looked in the gloomy interior, the beady black eyes of polar bears looked back at her, from the two long rows of cages. The bears paced and pawed at the bars, lifting their noses to smell the approaching intruders.

'In there!' John Bruce shouted, pointing to an empty holding pen at the far end.

Mandy and her mother manoeuvred their awkward burden through the narrow door and laid the cub gently on the concrete floor. The three men joined them in the cell, dragging the mother bear on the canvas stretcher.

Adam Hope was red-faced with the effort. 'She weighs a bit!' he exclaimed.

Mandy sank to her knees beside the cub. Putting out her hand, she lovingly stroked the little cub's face. Then she smoothed the soft fur around the baby's ears. Mandy looked at the mother bear. Her nose was working wildly as she tried to lift her head from the floor. Mandy hoped she could smell her cub. She didn't want the mother bear to think she had lost both her cubs. Mandy looked at the mother bear's huge feet. The pads were as rough as sandpaper, for traction on the ice, and the curved black claws were as sharp as razors. Every part of the polar bear was perfectly adapted to her unique living conditions.

'Good work, team!' John Bruce said cheerfully.

'Thanks for your help. We'll leave her for a bit and let her come round properly.'

'How long, Mr Bruce?' Mandy asked. 'I mean, how long will they have to stay here?'

'We'll ship them out as soon as the ice on the bay freezes over,' he replied. 'The temperature's dropping, so it should be within the next week.' He slammed and padlocked the door of the cell.

'What about the other cub?' Mandy asked, suddenly remembering the missing twin. 'Do you think they've managed to find it?'

'I hope so.' John Bruce glanced at his watch. 'But look, you lot have missed out on lunch and it's almost time for supper. It's been a long day. Why don't you go back, get settled at my house and have a bite to eat while I check with the team and see if they've found it yet?'

'Yes, please,' Mandy said eagerly. She was longing to know if the little cub had been found – it might even be on its way to the polar bear jail as they were talking.

In the cell behind her, the mother bear struggled to her feet. She was nosing her cub awake, licking its fur with her long red tongue. Mandy felt a surge of relief. At least one of the

cubs was all right. She just had to hope that the
other one was found soon . . .

A north wind had begun to blow, making it feel
even colder. The falling snow had thickened and
the sky was darkening.

'This bitter north wind is just what the polar
bears need. It will soon freeze the ice on the bay
if it keeps up,' Mr Bruce told them as they walked
over to the truck.

'Good,' said Mandy. She climbed into the back
seat beside her dad, while her mum joined John
Bruce and Mike in the front. The wind tugged at
the heavy rear door as Mandy struggled to shut
it. An iced-over Hudson Bay was exactly what she
longed for, so the bears could be set free to hunt
for food.

As they pulled away, John Bruce unclipped the
radio from the dashboard of the truck and put
out a call to his colleagues. A loud, crackling voice
replied, confirming that they were still looking
for the cub. Mandy gripped her dad's hand with
anxiety, and caught Mr Bruce's eye in the rearview
mirror.

'They'll find it,' he assured her, as he steered

the truck on to the main road. 'My team are used to finding bears in this town.'

But during the three-mile journey back to the Bruces' house, Mandy couldn't help feeling worried.

It was a great relief to Mandy to take off her heavy coat and boots and to flex her fingers free of the fur-lined mittens. In the warmth of the Bruces' kitchen, her freezing toes at last started to thaw.

Mrs Bruce ladled a spoonful of vegetable soup into a bowl, then buttered a thick slice of bread. 'There,' she smiled, handing the bowl to Mandy. 'Try some of my famous soup, for now. I'll cook a proper meal in a bit.' Hamish, in his basket by the fire, pricked up his ears. Seconds later, there was a loud knocking at the front door. Hamish yapped, but made no attempt to get up.

'I'll go,' said John Bruce. 'It's probably Bill and Dale.' He went out and shut the door to the front hall.

'Oh, yum. Thanks,' Mandy said gratefully, placing the bowl of soup on the kitchen counter. She propped herself on a stool next to Alicia and tucked in. The soup was scalding, but delicious.

'Great soup!' Mr Hope said approvingly, from the small table at the other end of the room.

'Hmm, it *is* good,' Emily Hope agreed. She was sitting in an armchair, and her feet were spread out towards the welcome warmth of the electric fire. From time to time, the shutters at the window rattled in the fierce wind. The sound of muffled voices drifted in from the hallway. At last Mr Bruce came back in.

'Any luck?' Alicia looked up expectantly. 'With the cub, I mean.'

'There's no sign of the little one. The team have given up the search for the night,' John Bruce told her. 'The lads came by to tell me which areas they've covered.' He looked concerned.

'It's snowing hard,' Mrs Bruce remarked, looking out of the big window in the kitchen. 'All tracks will be covered by now, anyway.'

'Will they start looking again tomorrow?' Mandy asked.

'Of course they will.' John Bruce nodded. 'First thing.'

'Is there room for us in the search party?' Adam Hope asked.

Mandy looked across at her dad and smiled

gratefully. He must have guessed how much Mandy wanted to look for the cub.

'We'd be glad to have you with us,' said John Bruce. 'Sunrise is around eight-thirty at the moment, so you won't have to get up early,' he added, winking at Mandy.

Mandy grinned back at him. She didn't mind how early she had to get up.

'Who wants a game of Monopoly?' Alicia suggested.

Mandy shrugged. She didn't really feel like playing games. She couldn't stop worrying about the polar bear cub. Had he been able to find shelter from the storm? What if he was frightened? Mandy grew more anxious about him with each passing minute. She could hardly wait for morning to come, when they could start their search again.

Seven

Mandy was staying in Alicia's room and they talked in low voices long into the night. Hamish, lost in a dream, grunted and twitched in his basket.

'He's dreaming about that polar bear!' Mandy laughed.

'Let's not think about the cub any more,' Alicia suggested, pulling her quilt up to her chin. 'Thinking won't help.'

Mandy was finding it hard to relax and go to sleep. Alicia kept Mandy's mind off the lost cub by telling her stories about her life in Manitoba.

She learned about the dog sled trials, and how the Inuit people survived during the winter months further north of Churchill. But, however hard they tried, they kept getting back to the subject of the polar bears.

'Where do you think the cub will go? In the storm, I mean?' Mandy asked Alicia.

'I expect he'll try and find shelter somewhere,' Alicia said hopefully. 'He may even stay close to the area where he ran off, believing that his mother will come and find him,' she added.

The girls fell silent. Mandy stared up at the sloping ceiling of the room, listening to the whistle of the wind outside. Soon she could tell from Alicia's steady breathing that her friend had fallen asleep. But Mandy stayed awake for a long time, hoping that the polar bear cub had found a sheltered place for the night.

When the watery sun struggled above the horizon the next morning, thick flakes of snow were still spiralling steadily downward, blurring the outlines of the little town. Mandy and Alicia wriggled out of bed and dressed quickly, eager to set out in search of the missing cub.

Over a breakfast of hot chocolate and toast, John Bruce filled them in on the search schedule. He was going to take Mandy and Alicia with him in the truck, and Mike and Bill would collect Mandy's mum and dad in the Land-rover, to search a different area. In spite of her anxiety, Mandy couldn't help feeling excited at the prospect of joining the polar team again.

'It feels as though it should be Christmas,' she said to Alicia as they stepped outside, well wrapped in several layers of thick clothes. Everything was coated with soft, powdery snow, sparkling with frost and tinged pink by the rising sun.

'Well, it's not – but it *is* Hallowe'en!' Alicia smiled. 'And I love it!'

'Come on, you two. Who's coming with me?' John Bruce drummed his fist on the roof of the truck.

Alicia looked at Mandy. 'We are!' they said at the same moment, bounding through the snow with Hamish at their heels.

'Bye!' yelled Adam Hope from the doorstep of the Bruces' house. He had a crust of toast in his hand. He and Mandy's mum were waiting for Mike and Bill to pick them up.

Emily Hope appeared beside her husband, holding a steaming mug of coffee. 'Best of luck finding the cub!' she called. 'We'll see you later!'

As they drove through Churchill, Mandy saw that the wind had swept the fresh snow into high, wave-shaped drifts. Children were out and about already, scooting along on sleds, carving out tunnels and building snowmen. Mandy was half-tempted to watch, but already her eyes were seeking out the places a small polar bear cub might be using for shelter.

'I'm going to head out in the direction of the bay,' Mr Bruce told them. 'That's about as far as the cub could have ranged. Then we'll start working our way back to town.'

'Right,' Alicia said, sitting up very straight in her seat. Hamish licked the last buttery traces of breakfast from her fingers.

'I can't believe how much snow has fallen,' Mandy remarked. 'Does it mean that the bay will have frozen over?'

'Not yet, lass,' Mr Bruce shook his head. 'That

will depend on the temperature, not on the snow.'

'Oh,' Mandy said and, once again, she silently willed the temperature to fall.

Time ticked by as Mr Bruce patiently cruised the outskirts of the town, looking left and right as he drove. But there was no sign of the cub. In the distance, Mandy spotted some of the other wildlife officers, trudging among the rocks on the freezing tundra, looking into crevices that could house a small animal. Mandy wondered if her mum and dad were with them.

Suddenly, Mr Bruce braked sharply. They were heading back into the town and were passing a collection of rundown wooden buildings. In the pristine snow, a set of small pawprints was clearly visible. Mandy's heart began to beat faster.

'Quick! Jump out!' Alicia cried, nudging Mandy in the ribs. 'This looks promising.'

Mr Bruce picked up a small plastic container which was on the dashboard of the truck. It held a filled syringe. Mandy guessed this was a small dose of tranquilliser, like the one her dad had used on the other cub. She and Alicia followed John Bruce as he tracked the prints away from the edge of the road, towards the wooden building. The prints were easily small enough to have been made by a young bear cub. Mr Bruce turned and gave the girls a thumbs-up sign, motioning for them to be absolutely quiet. Mandy hoped that Hamish wouldn't choose this moment to let off a volley of yapping from inside the truck.

The neat little impressions in the snow led inside a shed. The door hung ajar on rusted hinges. John Bruce pushed the door wider as slowly and noiselessly as possible. Right away, Mandy could hear the curious chomping of a small jaw. Her heart tightened in her chest.

'It's the cub!' Alicia mouthed at Mandy, her eyes wide as she stepped into the shed behind her dad.

Mandy went in after Mr Bruce and Alicia, her excitement mounting. It took a moment for her eyes to become accustomed to the gloom, and then she saw the little cub.

It was crouched under a plank of wood that had once served as a shelf. The plank had collapsed at one end, making a convenient, dry hiding place for a frightened polar bear. The cub peeped out at the approaching strangers, blinking.

John Bruce sank to his haunches and took a

good, long look at the cub. 'What a state you're in!' he said softly to the grimy little bear.

Mandy's heart turned over at the sight of the forlorn animal. It seemed smaller than the other cub, and a lot thinner. She longed to rush forward and give it a hug, but she knew that even though it was small, it could still be aggressive and she didn't want to alarm it.

She watched as Mr Bruce inched towards the cub, talking in a low voice. The little bear had backed so far into the corner that its hindlegs were

pressed up against the shed wall. It growled and chomped as it watched the man getting closer.

'There, now . . .' Mr Bruce whispered. He reached out a hand to try and grab the cub, but it had other ideas. It sprang from under the plank, jumping clear of John Bruce's outstretched hand. As it made a dash for the open door of the shed, Alicia blocked the way. In panic, the cub veered to the right. Mandy gasped as she saw it run straight into the prongs of a rusty pitchfork propped against a pile of wood.

The cub gave a grunt and a squeal. Bright red blood began to seep into its cream-coloured coat. The tiny cub had impaled itself on the metal prong of the fork. The spike had gone into its chest, and was holding it fast. Mandy watched as John Bruce instantly sized up the situation.

'I've got you,' he said soothingly, as he took the syringe out of the plastic case. He bent down and swiftly injected the tranquilliser into the cub's neck.

The wounded cub struggled briefly against the spike that held him. Mandy waited anxiously for the drug to take effect. Soon the bear closed his eyes and his body began to sag.

In a trice, John Bruce had eased the tip of the prong out of his flesh. The wound gaped. 'Have either of you . . .' he began, looking around. But Mandy knew exactly what he was going to ask for. She unwound a silky scarf her mother had lent her to stop the woolly neck of her jumper itching. John Bruce took it gratefully and bound it tightly under the cub's front leg and across his back.

Free of the spike, the bear had slumped to the floor. 'He's still losing blood,' John Bruce said. 'We'll have to get him back for treatment – and fast – or he'll die.'

'I wish Mum and Dad were here,' Mandy murmured, knowing that her father rarely travelled without his veterinary bag.

'Well, at least they're not far away,' John Bruce said calmly. 'The vet I normally use is some distance from here. It'll be quicker to get to your parents. Come on, let's get the cub to the truck. I'll radio your parents when we're on our way.'

Eight

Mandy and Alicia held the cub between them as John Bruce drove back to the town centre. As they raced along the snowy roads, Mr Bruce called Mike on the radio and asked him to take Mr and Mrs Hope back to the Bruces' house as quickly as possible. Mandy felt very relieved as soon as she knew her mum and dad were on their way to meet them. Meanwhile, the polar bear cub lay limply, spread out across the laps of the girls. His breathing was fast and shallow, and the wound was still bleeding in spite of the scarf.

Hamish was sitting in the passenger footwell.

Alicia reached down to stroke him. The Scottie quivered all over, straining to sniff at the cub.

'No, Hamish,' Alicia told him firmly. 'Keep still!'

'Keep the palm of your hand pressed against that wound,' Mr Bruce instructed Mandy. She nodded, looking down at the skinny cub. It whimpered in its sleep. Mandy hoped her mum and dad would be able to help the little bear.

'Hurry, Mr Bruce,' Mandy pleaded, as they turned into the main street.

'We're nearly there,' he told her.

The town's wide, white main street was busy with Saturday morning traffic. Sleds and snowmobiles were everywhere, and the tundra buggy driver was shepherding a line of tourists on board the bus.

'Hurry up!' Mandy muttered under her breath, as a plump elderly man levered himself slowly aboard, just in front of them.

Mr Bruce steered the truck past the tourists and pulled up sharply. Mandy noticed with relief that they were outside number 43.

'Stay in the truck. I'll see if Adam and Emily are back,' John Bruce said. He got out and took the stairs to the front door in a single leap. Alicia and Mandy exchanged anxious glances.

'Here's my dad,' Mandy said, as Mr Bruce reappeared with Adam Hope close behind him. 'Thank goodness.'

Mr Hope opened the door on Mandy's side and looked in. 'Poor thing,' he murmured as he gently lifted the cub out. The cub's head lolled. 'Mandy, get my bag, will you, love?'

Mandy raced indoors, Alicia behind her. Together they ran to the little back bedroom where Mr and Mrs Hope had slept, and found the black bag beside the bed. Then they hurried back to the living-room, where Adam Hope was standing with the cub in his arms. Mandy carried the bag into the kitchen area, while Alicia went and sat down on the sofa with Hamish, to keep him out of the way.

John Bruce spread a plastic tablecloth across the kitchen counter and Mr Hope placed the cub on to it.

'I'll need some sterile instruments,' Adam Hope said, peering into the bear's wound.

'They'll have everything you need over at the research unit,' John Bruce said. 'We could take the bear over there.'

But Mandy's dad shook his head. 'I don't want to move this little chap just now,' he said gravely. 'Can you get the equipment for me, and bring it here?'

'Sure,' Mr Bruce agreed. 'That's no problem. It's only a five-minute drive from here.'

'Good.' Mr Hope nodded. 'Thanks, John.' He took a small bottle of special soap from his bag and began scrubbing his hands under the tap at the kitchen sink.

Mandy found a roll of wrapped paper towels and handed him one. 'Is he going to be OK, Dad?' she asked softly.

'His breathing is noisy,' Adam Hope said, drying his hands thoroughly. 'I can't be sure just yet, love. I hope he hasn't damaged a lung.'

'You mean he could be seriously hurt?' Mandy said, her heart sinking.

'It's only a possibility,' Mr Hope said gently. 'I need to take a look at him first.'

While they were waiting for Mr Bruce to return, Adam Hope began clipping away the bloodied fur round the wound in the cub's chest. Then he injected a local anaesthetic into the skin next to the wound.

'It's so he won't feel any pain when he wakes up,' he explained.

Mandy nodded. She'd watched her parents operate so many times, she understood most of the procedures. All she cared about was making the little cub better. She stroked the sleeping cub's soft head, trying to comfort him.

It seemed an age before John Bruce came back, carrying a small pack of surgical instruments in a sterile wrap.

'Thanks, John,' Mr Hope said, unwrapping the instruments and selecting one.

Emily Hope joined them. She had been taking a shower after her cold morning on the tundra. 'What on earth happened?' she asked Mandy, frowning.

'We found the cub in a shed,' Mandy explained. 'But he was scared and he ran into a pitchfork.'

'Right into one of the prongs,' John Bruce joined in.

Mandy's mum looked concerned.

There was silence as Adam Hope carefully inspected the wound. 'It's not very deep,' he announced, straightening up. 'And he hasn't damaged the lung,' he added thankfully.

Mandy breathed a sigh of relief. She stood close to the cub while her dad used a syringe to flush out the messy wound. Then he began to stitch it closed.

As Mandy watched, she wondered if she should give the cub a name. It seemed odd to call it 'him' all the time. With one last stroke of the cub's furry head, she tiptoed away from the counter and joined Alicia at the other end of the room. 'Let's think of a name for the cub,' Mandy whispered.

'Good idea!' Alicia replied softly.

They thought for a moment.

'How about Solo, as he's been wandering around on his own?' suggested Alicia.

'But he's not on his own any more,' Mandy pointed out. She frowned. 'I know, how about Polo?'

'Yes, that really suits him,' Alicia agreed, looking across at the kitchen counter where Adam Hope was still bending over the cub's motionless body. She glanced back at Mandy. 'He *will* be OK, won't he?' she asked.

'I hope so,' said Mandy seriously. 'If anyone can help him, my dad can.'

Just then, Mr Hope straightened up and put

down the needle he was holding. 'All done,' he said, sounding satisfied.

'Great. Shall we take the little fellow down to the jail to join his mother now, Adam?' asked John Bruce.

'No, I don't think so.' Mandy's dad shook his head. 'There's a chance that the wound may be infected. I'm going to give him a shot of antibiotic now. Will it be possible to keep him in isolation and watch him carefully over the next few days?'

'There's a unit at the Research Station,' John Bruce said. 'I'll take him down there.'

'I'd go right away,' Adam Hope urged as the bear cub started to twitch and grunt very softly. 'That sedative is starting to wear off.'

Mandy and Alicia watched Mr Bruce carry Polo out to the truck. Emily Hope joined them, and put her arms round Mandy. Mandy hugged her mum back. She felt desperately sad for the tiny cub, who looked fragile and helpless in John Bruce's arms.

'Can I feed Polo?' She looked up at her mum. 'With a bottle? He'll be needing milk!'

'But you know that Mr Bruce said we have to keep contact between humans and polar bears to a minimum,' Emily Hope reminded her gently. 'Polo's a wild animal. A strong smell of humans on his fur may cause his mother to reject him.'

'I know, but he's starving – and weak, and thin!' Mandy protested. She understood what her mum was saying, but it was so hard to leave the little cub feeling hungry as well as scared.

'As soon as he's well enough, we'll put him back with his mum. Let's hope he can feed from her.' Emily Hope was firm. She squeezed Mandy's shoulders. 'Come on, love,' she said. 'Let's go inside and get some lunch before we freeze.'

As Mandy began to help her parents pack away and clean up the kitchen, she wondered just how long Polo would have to wait before he could join his mother and sister. Judging by his limp, helpless state, Mandy didn't think he could wait very long.

There was nothing more to be done for Polo, so after lunch Mandy joined Alicia in the sitting area. Hamish leaped off Alicia's lap to greet her, his whole body wagging with pleasure.

'We might as well get ready for Hallowe'en,' Alicia said. 'At least it will keep our minds off Polo.'

Mandy felt like shaking her head. She really didn't feel like celebrating anything, not while Polo lay fighting for his life in the research unit. She had even forgotten that today was October the thirty-first. But Alicia was looking so enthusiastic about Hallowe'en that Mandy didn't have the heart to let her down. 'Right,' she said brightly, summoning a smile. 'Let's get started.'

Between them, they rolled a fat, round pumpkin weighing about four and a half kilos out of the larder and across the kitchen floor. Alicia fetched a long serrated knife while Mandy spread newspaper around them. When the knife had been drawn through the top of the pumpkin in a full circle, Mandy plucked the lid off neatly, by the stem.

'Do you carve jack-o-lanterns in England?' Alicia asked, fetching two metal spoons from a drawer.

'Jack-o-what?' Mandy echoed, puzzled.

'It's what we call hollowed-out pumpkins,' Alicia explained.

'Oh, right. Well, some people do,' Mandy said, pausing to scrape out a stubborn chunk of pumpkin flesh, 'but it's not such a big holiday at home as it is over here.' She tapped the spoonful

of pumpkin into the waiting bowl, and resumed her attack.

When the sticky orange contents had been scooped out and saved for Mrs Bruce's pumpkin pie, Alicia drew a ferocious face on the skin in pen, then carved it out with Mandy's help. The final touch was the placing of a candle inside the hollow pumpkin. Alicia lit it, and they stood back to admire their handiwork as the fierce face began to glow. The flame flickered behind the triangular eyes and grinning mouth.

'It looks great,' Alicia said, sounding pleased.

'I'll go and put it out on the front doorstep. Then, we'll get dressed for trick-or-treating.'

'Hallowe'en, rather inconveniently, falls smack in the middle of the polar bear season,' John Bruce said with a wry smile, as he walked into town with Mandy and Alicia. 'Our Bear Patrol has to be extra vigilant.'

Mandy tilted the witch's hat she wore so she could peer out from under the wide brim. 'What will you do tonight that's different?' she asked.

'We'll carry loaded tranquillising guns and rifles, just in case,' Mr Bruce said. 'We can't really afford to take any chances when there are so many people about.'

'Also, there are the searchlights – see, there?' Beside her, Alicia pointed to the sky.

'Oh, yes!' Mandy was impressed. Bright beams of white light pierced the darkness.

'Several vehicles are patrolling the town, watching for bears,' Mr Bruce assured them. 'You'll be absolutely safe.'

Mandy smiled at him. She was as snug as could be in her costume. Mrs Bruce had found it in their box of dressing-up clothes, and it was lined with fleecy material for extra warmth.

Alicia used the flashlight she carried to keep an eye on Hamish. The Scottie was wearing a little tartan coat buttoned under his tummy. He trotted along on his lead, his head held high.

'I was a monster last year,' Alicia told Mandy. 'But my costume was so good I made one of the little children cry!' This year, she was wearing a dramatic witch's cloak, decorated with silver moons and stars which shimmered in the street lights.

All along the street, jack-o-lanterns flickered in the icy air. Shadowy figures raced through the darkness up ahead – ghosts and witches of every description. Mandy saw a couple of small children dressed as polar bears, too.

John Bruce smiled and waved to someone he knew. 'This is a very well-drilled operation,' he told Mandy. 'All my men are out to make certain the bears don't come too close to the town, so there's no need to worry.'

'I'm not worried at all,' Mandy reassured him.

But Mandy was glad he was with them. Her parents had decided to use the evening to catch up on some work, and John Bruce had insisted the girls were chaperoned. Mandy was thrilled to be a part of the celebration, along with the whole town it seemed, making Churchill look very festive. The brightly lit streets were a huge contrast to the vast, echoing emptiness of the dark tundra around them.

Alicia led Mandy from house to house. Every house they visited had entered wholeheartedly into the spirit of the holiday. Rubber spiders and black cats danced in every window. Baskets and bowls brimming with sweets, chocolates and cookies were offered at each door. It was left to Mr Bruce to help carry the sack-load they collected.

After the tenth house, which was down a narrow road off the main street, the bitter cold was beginning to penetrate Mandy's costume. Gratefully, she accepted a cup of hot chocolate on the doorstep of someone's house. 'How are we going to eat all of these sweets?' she asked Alicia. 'It will take a whole year to . . .'

She was interrupted by a series of sharp popping noises from several streets away. Hamish jumped, and tried to get under the long, fleece-lined costume Alicia was wearing.

'Is that fireworks?' Mandy asked, looking up at the sky.

'Guns,' Alicia answered, frowning. 'Those noises are made by special shells which they fire to scare away the bears.'

'But . . . that means . . . ?' Mandy gasped.

'Yep,' Alicia answered cheerfully. 'There's a bear about.'

Mr Bruce spoke into his radio. 'North Street?' he said. 'How many men have you got stationed up there? Two? That should be fine.'

There was a volley of firing, crackling across the night sky. Mandy put her gloved hands over her ears. Alicia hunched her shoulders and pulled a face.

'I'm going to go over and see what's happening, girls,' Mr Bruce said. 'I won't be long. They might need my help. OK?'

'OK,' said Alicia. 'I never get used to the noise of the shells,' she confessed to Mandy, as her father jogged away down the street. Then she gasped. 'Oh! *Hamish!*'

'What?' said Mandy, uncovering her ears. She'd been gazing up at the flares shooting into the sky. She looked down at the little dog, who was quivering on the ground.

'Hamish!' Alicia said again urgently. 'Oh, Mandy, I think the noise of the firing has frightened him into having a fit!'

Hamish was lying in the snow by Alicia's feet. In the beam of Alicia's flashlight, Mandy could see his lips were pulled back over his teeth. It looked as if Hamish was snarling. His back legs were stretched out in the snow, rigid, and his sides heaved.

'Help me, Mandy,' Alicia begged. 'I've not seen Hamish so bad before.'

'You stay here with Hamish,' Mandy said quickly, trying to calm her friend. 'I'll run and fetch my mum or dad.'

Hamish's neck was twisted at an impossible angle and his body had begun to shudder. 'Hurry, Mandy,' Alicia pleaded.

Mandy grabbed Alicia's flashlight and began to run.

She fled back the way they had come. The icy crust that had formed on the surface of last night's snow crackled and crunched under her feet. It was ankle-deep, which made it harder to hurry.

She was shivering with cold, but hardly noticed as she was so worried about Hamish.

Mandy knew she must not get lost. There were very few landmarks, no brightly-lit corner shops or public buildings that she had taken note of. The beam of the torch showed her only the sort of places a polar bear might hide, empty wooden buildings standing on stilts. Mandy willed her frozen feet to go faster. The skirt of her costume swirled about her legs as she plunged on through the snow. Somewhere in the next street she could hear the gleeful shouts of children.

Mandy reached a T-junction. She stopped, out of breath, uncertain for a moment which way to go. With every passing second, she was aware of Alicia sitting in the street waiting for help. As she looked anxiously up and down the street, she heard a shout behind her.

Mandy swung the torch in the direction of the sound. The beam picked out a man wearing a padded navy coat and matching trousers. He had just jumped out of a gleaming white four-wheel drive which had the Royal Canadian Mounted Police logo on the doors. 'Are you OK?' he called.

'I'm fine,' Mandy puffed. 'But . . .'

'It's very dangerous to be out on the streets alone, in the dark,' the man said sharply.

'I know,' Mandy said, 'but my friend needs help. Her dog is having an epileptic fit.' She looked around her. 'And now I'm not sure which way to go!'

'Where are you headed?' asked the officer.

'I'm trying to reach her house,' Mandy explained. 'My parents are there. Can you tell me which way is Main Street East? I'm looking for number 43.'

'John Bruce's house?' he asked her.

'Yes, please, I have to hurry!' Mandy was growing frantic.

'You're nearly there,' the officer told her. 'Just go round that corner, and it's the second house on the left.' He looked past her and pointed. 'You'll be there in less than a minute.'

'Thanks!' Mandy gasped. She wheeled about and leaped through the snow with renewed energy. 'Hang on, Hamish . . .' she muttered to herself. 'Hang on, Alicia. Help is on the way.'

Nine

A small crowd of people had gathered around Alicia by the time Mandy and her dad returned. A tall woman with long dark hair stood next to her, looking down anxiously.

'Coming through!' Adam Hope called, forging a path through the onlookers with his vet's bag in his hand.

Alicia was sitting on the doorstep with the little dog cradled in her lap. 'I'm so worried,' she began as soon as she saw Mr Hope. 'Thank goodness you're here.'

'She wouldn't come in the house,' the dark-haired woman told Mandy's dad, waving her hands in frustration. 'We tried to get her to bring the little dog inside but . . .'

'That was kind of you,' Adam Hope said, bending down, 'but Alicia was quite right not to move him. If you'll all move back just a bit, please. Now, let's take a look at you, Hamish.'

Mandy knelt beside Alicia to get a better look at the dog. He was wrapped in a blanket that someone had brought for him, with just his face peeping out.

'The fit was really bad,' Alicia said. 'He was shaking and shuddering and his legs were all stiff, for about five minutes.' Hamish looked up at Mr Hope. The Scottie's eyes were glassy and strange. 'I thought he had stopped breathing and there was saliva pouring out of his mouth,' Alicia went on.

Mandy felt very sorry for her friend. It must have been awful to watch her dog in so much distress.

Adam Hope unfolded the blanket and placed his stethoscope over Hamish's heart. Then he shone a little torch into each of his eyes. Hamish didn't seem to like it much, and he wriggled in

Alicia's arms. Mr Hope took out a syringe from his bag. 'This will help him to relax,' he explained, slipping the needle into the muscle at the back of the little dog's neck.

Within a few moments, Hamish's eyes closed. He began to snore softly and Mandy tucked the blanket snugly round him.

Now that help had arrived, the crowd began to drift away and the street fell quiet. There were no more firecracker shells to be heard, and the lights that had lit up the sky had stopped too.

Mandy saw that the hem of Alicia's dress was soaked with melted snow, and she was shivering violently. Only about fifteen minutes had passed since Mandy had left her to dash home, yet to Alicia it must have seemed more like an hour.

'Dad, we should get Alicia home. Can we move Hamish?' Mandy asked.

'Yes, I think so.' Adam Hope looked at Hamish's gums. 'A nice, healthy pink,' he said. 'He seems fine again. Let me lift him for you, Alicia.'

Hamish went quietly into Adam Hope's arms and Mandy helped Alicia to her feet.

'Thanks for fetching your dad,' Alicia said. 'Hamish means the world to me.'

Mandy nodded and smiled. She could see how much Alicia loved her little dog.

'Alicia! Adam!' John Bruce was striding up the street towards them. He was still carrying the bag of sweets the girls had collected. 'Is everything all right?'

'Dad!' Alicia said. 'Hamish had a fit and Mandy had to go and get Mr Hope!'

Mr Bruce put an arm round his daughter and looked closely at the dog. 'He's all right now, though, Adam?'

'He's fine, but I'd like to keep an eye on him,' Mandy's dad said.

'Poor wee chap,' said Mr Bruce. He reached out and ruffled Hamish's ears with his gloved hand.

'What happened?' asked Mandy. 'Was there a bear?' She took Alicia's arm and they began to walk back along the snowy street.

John Bruce fell into step beside them. 'There sure was,' he said. 'He wandered off, back to the tundra, once the firecrackers went off.'

'Thank goodness for that!' said Alicia. 'Now, let's get home and make Hamish comfortable. Then we can eat some of that candy!'

*   *   *

Hamish lay meekly in his basket beside the fire in the living-room. He seemed listless and subdued. He wouldn't even lift his head for his favourite treat, a piece of chicken.

Mandy stroked his head. 'Will it happen again?' she asked her mum, who was kneeling beside her on the hearthrug. 'I mean, soon?'

'Usually not,' Mrs Hope said. 'From what Alicia has told me, it seems Hamish has had mild epilepsy in the past, but tonight's fit was a little more complex. It seems to have affected the whole of his body, poor boy.'

Alicia came over to join them, her cheeks flushed red after a hot shower. She was wearing a thick fluffy robe and her hair was wrapped in a towel. 'How long will he be like this?' she asked, looking down anxiously at the limp little dog.

'He might be restless or unresponsive for a few days, Alicia,' Mandy's mum warned. 'But we've done everything we can. He just needs a bit of TLC now.'

Alicia smiled. 'I'll look after him,' she promised.

'Well, it's time for my bed,' John Bruce announced. 'I'm beat.' He folded the newspaper he had been reading and clambered to his feet from the comfortable sofa.

'Me too,' said Mrs Hope. She looked at her husband. 'Adam, are you coming now?'

'Actually, I'd like to take a look at Polo in the research unit before I turn in. Is that OK with you, John?'

'Sure,' said Mr Bruce. 'You go ahead, Adam. You know the code for the alarm. The keypad is just inside the door.' He groped in his pocket and tossed Mr Hope the keys to the unit's front door. 'See you in the morning.'

Mandy scrambled to her feet. 'May I come, Dad?' she asked.

Adam Hope glanced at his wife, then smiled. 'OK, love. Alicia?'

'No, thanks.' Alicia shook her head. 'I think I'd better stay with Hamish. Give Polo my love, Mandy.'

'I will.' Mandy shrugged on her padded jacket and pulled up the hood. She pictured the tiny polar bear cub, limp and bleeding after his accident. Her heart began to beat faster. She crossed her fingers inside her mittens. Oh, please, *please*, let Polo be well!

* * *

The Hopes' rented Jeep was parked just outside the Bruces' house. A sheet of ice had already formed across the windscreen. Mr Hope scrabbled around in the glove compartment and found an ice scraper. Mandy climbed into the passenger seat and waited while her father chipped away. Even inside her thick gloves, her fingers were turning numb with cold. Surely soon, very soon, the ice over Hudson Bay would be solid enough for the Churchill bears to begin their journey north.

'Brrr!' Adam Hope jumped into the driving seat. 'I've never experienced cold like this.'

'Me neither,' said Mandy. 'I dreamed last night of that time we were in Africa. I could feel the hot sun on my back. It was lovely! I bet the people round here can't wait for spring.'

'Yes, indeed. But it's not just the animals which have adapted to this climate,' Mr Hope pointed out, as he bumped off the icy pavement and on to the road. 'And as John said, they don't feel the cold until it's fifty below freezing!'

'Dad?' Mandy's mind was wandering back to the little cub. 'What'll happen to Polo if he's not well enough to travel north with his mother?'

Adam Hope sighed. 'I don't know, Mandy, love,' he replied honestly. 'Orphaned polar bear cubs are usually sent to a zoo, if they're too young to survive in the wild.'

'A zoo!' Mandy exclaimed. 'But this is where Polo belongs! It would be a shame to take him away from the ice.'

Adam Hope put a gentle hand on Mandy's knee. 'Steady on,' he cautioned. 'Let's not jump to any conclusions until we see how the little chap is getting on, shall we?'

It was pitch dark inside the research unit building. Mandy followed her father along the shadowy corridors, reading the door signs by the light of a powerful torch.

'Veterinary Research,' Adam Hope read at last. 'He's in here.' He unlocked the door and felt around on the wall inside for a light switch. The overhead fluorescent lighting seemed unnaturally bright to Mandy as it flooded the small square room.

Polo blinked and sat up. As soon as he saw the intruders, he gave a small hiss and began to whine.

He had been curled up asleep on an old towel inside a wire mesh cage which stood on a table in the centre of the room. He had knocked over his bowl of water, and the towel was wet.

Mandy approached gingerly. 'Hello, Polo,' she murmured. The bear backed away into the furthest corner of his enclosure, swaying his little head from side to side. Mandy heard the strange chewing sound that alarmed polar bears make. 'Don't worry, little one. We won't hurt you,' she whispered. 'We're going to make you better. Then we'll take you back to your mum.'

At the sound of her voice, Polo lowered his head and took a step towards Mandy, sniffing curiously. Mandy stayed very still, hardly daring to breathe. Was he beginning to trust her?

'He's looking a bit better,' Mandy's dad said quietly, coming up behind Mandy. 'He's certainly more alert than he was. I can't quite see the wound from this angle. Ah, there, he's turned round. Yes, so far, so good.'

'Good?' Mandy questioned eagerly. She peered at the long row of stitches in the little bear's chest, a row of black knots against his partly shaved chest. 'How do you mean, good?'

'Well, there's no swelling or redness around the injury, which means there's no infection starting,' Mr Hope explained. He bent down to get a closer look.

'I guess that's something.' Mandy sighed. She couldn't help thinking that Polo still looked a mess. His paws were black with filth from his run through the town, and his chest was matted with dried blood. There was blood on his nose and muzzle too.

'However, he *is* very thin,' Adam Hope went on, sounding serious. 'Really thin. I don't think . . .'

'What?' Mandy turned to him, suddenly feeling anxious.

'Well, I don't think he'll last much longer without a meal,' her dad said heavily.

'Oh, Dad!' Mandy gasped.

'Still, I don't think John Bruce and his team will stand by and watch Polo die of starvation, love.' Mr Hope straightened up and smiled at Mandy. 'All the wildlife officers have the bears' best interests at heart, and John knows what he's doing.'

'I know you're right. Polo's with the experts

now,' Mandy said, wishing she could reach into the cage and stroke the little cub. Even though she understood that looking after polar bears was completely different to anything she had experienced before, it did feel strange not to be able to give a starving animal a good meal. Mandy couldn't imagine letting any animals go hungry in the residential unit at Animal Ark! But, then, animals in Welford were not designed to go for several months of the year without eating anything, she reminded herself.

While Mandy and her dad were talking, Polo had moved a bit closer to the mesh. He lifted his head, so that he seemed to be looking directly at Mandy with his small black eyes. Quickly, she knelt down, hoping the little bear wouldn't scamper away to the farthest corner of the cage. Polo stayed where he was. He seemed calm now, and curious. For a few seconds, they looked deeply into one another's eyes. It was a thrilling moment for Mandy. Suddenly she felt that Polo understood that she, and the rest of the polar sheriff's team, were on his side.

'Goodnight, Polo,' she whispered as she stood up.

Her father put an arm around her. 'Try not to worry so much,' he said. 'Polo seems to be recovering quickly from his injury. If he doesn't start an infection, he'll soon be reunited with his mother – and then she'll be able to feed him.'

'Yes,' said Mandy, giving her father a small smile. 'You're right.'

'And you should be in bed!' Adam Hope added. 'It's after midnight! Come on, let's say goodbye to Polo and get some sleep.'

On Sunday morning, while Alicia was walking Hamish, Mandy caught up with her school work and found time to write a long e-mail to her friend, James, on Mr Bruce's computer.

When I next write to you, she ended her message, *I'll be able to tell you if Polo survived. It's almost all I can think about at the moment. He's the cutest little cub in the world, but he's sick and he's starving. We're crossing our fingers for him. You cross fingers for him too, and give Blackie a hug from me.*

After lunch, Mandy went with her mum and dad, Alicia and John Bruce to see Polo. Mandy and Alicia stood well back as Mr Bruce opened the door of the cage and held on to Polo, wearing leather gloves to protect him from the nervous cub's snapping teeth and sharp claws. Polo only struggled briefly before crouching down on the table and submitting to the careful examination.

Emily Hope gently prodded the area around the stitches, while Mandy's dad gave him an injection of an antibiotic drug. Mandy watched, spellbound, as the small white bear wriggled and growled softly.

Mrs Hope held him by the scruff of his neck.

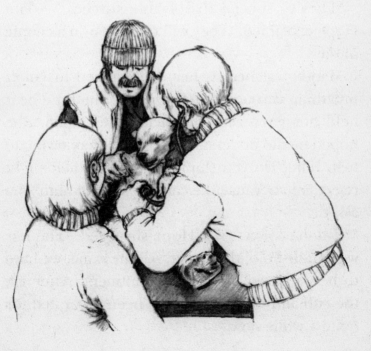

'He's in need of some food, Adam,' she commented. 'But he's got so much strength. I can barely hold him!'

Polo twisted in her grasp, scrabbling on the table's smooth surface with his furry paws. John Bruce adjusted his grip and held the little body still.

'What about the stitches?' Alicia asked, peering past her dad to look at Polo's chest. 'When will they come out?'

'They're special dissolvable stitches,' Adam Hope explained. 'They will disappear in a couple of days.'

Mandy watched as her dad listened to Polo's breathing through a stethoscope. The little bear held her gaze with his beady eyes again. She hoped he did understand that they were trying to help him. 'Do you think that his mother might reject Polo because she can smell us on him?' she asked.

'I don't know.' Mrs Hope shrugged. 'The less we handle Polo, the better. All the same, we have to be prepared for a disappointment. After all, the cub and his mother have been separated for quite a while now.'

Mandy felt her heart sink. Even though he was recovering from the wound, Polo still had a long way to go before he was safely back in the wild.

Adam Hope unhooked his stethoscope from his ears and stepped back from the table. Mr Bruce lifted Polo back into the cage, and shut the door firmly. The cub shook himself, like a dog coming out of water, and rubbed one eye with his big paw.

'His breathing's good,' Mr Hope said, sounding pleased. 'We'll just give him one more day, and then we'll let him go back to his mum.'

'Great!' Mandy said. She exchanged a delighted grin with Alicia.

'Come on, you two,' said Emily Hope. 'It's time to go back.' She handed Mandy her jacket and pushed open the door to the room. Mandy and Alicia went over to Polo's cage to say goodbye before following the others into the corridor.

When she stepped out into the icy afternoon air, Mandy saw that the sky was filled with deep purple clouds, hazy and low across the horizon. A gust of wind unwound Adam Hope's scarf and blew it across the carpark.

'Wow!' John Bruce looked around him. 'Looks

like there's going to be a storm.'

'More snow?' Emily Hope asked, fastening the hood of her jacket.

'Maybe,' Mr Bruce replied sounding thoughtful. '*Something's* coming, that's for sure!'

As they set out for the town centre, the first big flakes of snow began to fall.

During the night, the wind shifted from the south-west to the north-east, bringing with it ice and more snow. In Alicia's bedroom, Mandy snuggled deeper under her duvet and hugged her knees. The dim light of a lamp on the landing filtered in, and she could see that Hamish had jumped on to Alicia's bed. The little Scottie was curled into the crook of Alicia's arm, making tiny snuffling noises as he slept.

As Mandy slept, she dreamed she was taking Polo to Hudson Bay, to release him on to the ice. The sheet ice was rock-hard. Polo began to run and Mandy's spirits soared. She was smiling in her sleep when Alicia woke her.

'Pancakes,' Alicia said, stretching. 'That's what I feel like for breakfast. And then we'll go and visit Polo. OK?'

'Right.' Mandy grinned. She felt especially optimistic this morning. Her dream seemed like an omen – Polo would soon be free.

In the kitchen, Mandy and Alicia found Mr and Mrs Hope working side by side on John Bruce's laptop. Alicia's mum was at the other end of the table, drinking a mug of coffee as she scanned the morning papers.

'And what time do you call this?' Adam Hope asked with mock severity, tapping playfully on his wristwatch.

'School holiday time!' Alicia answered cheerfully. 'Two more days of it! Where's Dad?'

'He had to go out, Alicia,' Mrs Bruce told her. 'He's got some work to do in the office.'

'Oh, right,' said Alicia, as she began to take the pancake ingredients out of the cupboard.

'I heard the storm in the night,' Mandy said.

'It's still going on,' Mr Hope told her. 'Take a look outside.'

Mandy went to the window. She could hardly see across the street. Thick snow flakes were being buffeted around by the wind. They were spiralling into the pane and freezing there, as soon as they touched the cold glass.

'I'm glad I'm not out there!' said Mandy, shivering dramatically. Then she yawned.

'Hmm,' observed her father. 'Still sleepy? After that lie-in? Well, some of us have to do a little work around here. I've been to check on Polo this morning already.'

Mandy spun round from the window. 'Why didn't you say? How is he?' she demanded, instantly feeling wide awake.

'In good health,' Mrs Hope announced.

'Polo is ready to join his mum!' Adam Hope added, grinning.

'Oh, thank goodness,' Mandy sighed.

'Mr Bruce is going to take Polo to the jail when he gets back,' Mr Hope went on.

'Can we go along?' Mandy asked. Beside her, Alicia nodded enthusiastically.

'I'd like to see him try and stop you,' Adam Hope remarked with a smile.

It was agony having to wait for Mr Bruce's return. Mandy ate far too many pancakes drenched in maple syrup. She lay in a warm bath, then played cards with Alicia – until finally they heard the return of Mr Bruce's truck. Mandy and Alicia barely gave him time to have a cup of coffee before they bustled him back into his outdoor clothing, both as eager as each other to see Polo reunited with his family. Mandy's mum and dad offered to go too, but Mr Bruce told them he could manage on his own. Also, too many people might upset the mother bear and make her more likely to reject the cub.

Once they reached the research centre, John Bruce took charge of Polo's transportation to the polar bear jail. First, he injected the cub with a small dose of tranquilliser, then he lifted him on to a canvas sheet and carried him out to the truck. Polo lay quietly in a small white heap. The snow quickly began to cover him, like a blanket. Mandy wanted to say goodbye, but John Bruce wouldn't allow either of the girls near him this time.

'Let him be,' he said gently. 'His mother will be confused if her cub comes back smelling of you two!'

Mandy knew that Mr Bruce was right. She didn't want to do anything to harm Polo's chances of being accepted by his mother. Trembling with anticipation, she got into the cab beside Alicia and they set off for the jail.

The snow made driving difficult. The truck's windscreen wipers battled to cope with the ice being dumped on the glass. Several times a powerful gust of wind buffeted the vehicle, making John Bruce whistle through his teeth and raise a surprised eyebrow as he gripped the steering wheel and struggled to keep the truck straight.

By the time they reached the polar jail, Polo was wet through and much whiter than before, washed clean by the deluge of snow and sleet. He was still dozy, but awake. John Bruce lifted the sleepy cub out of the truck and into his arms, like a baby.

'I'm going to allow you girls inside to watch,' he told them, as he strode towards the jail. 'It's against regulations, as you well know, Alicia. But I know you're both dying to see the cub back with his mother.'

'Oh, yes please!' Mandy cried. She was longing to know if Polo's mother was going to be pleased to see him. She felt a shiver run down her spine. What if the bear rejected him? What would happen to Polo then?

As the big metal door to the jail swung open,

Mandy braced herself for the strong smell of many polar bears confined in a small space. Of the twenty-three cells in the jail, sixteen were now full. A holding pen next to Polo's mother had been made ready for the little cub.

'The door between them can be opened from outside,' John Bruce explained as he strode across the concrete floor with Polo in his arms. 'I want to see how she reacts to him first.'

Alicia opened the door to the pen, and her dad pushed Polo in. The cub lay limply on the floor in the middle of the cell, blinking sleepily. In the next door pen, the mother bear watched them curiously, sniffing at them suspiciously with her head held high.

Mandy felt her excitement growing. This was the moment she had been waiting for. After all he had been through, little Polo at last had the chance to return to the care of his mother. Surely she would know him by his scent, even if he had been missing for a few days? 'Go on, Polo,' Mandy urged the little polar bear silently. 'Get up and go to your mum!'

The cub was clearly disorientated. At first, he didn't even try to get up. He lay there looking slowly around him, sniffing hard at the dank air in the small cell. The smell was overpowering, and Mandy had to force herself not to make a dash for the fresh air outside. She hunched down just outside the pen next to Alicia, tucking her nose into her woollen scarf.

Polo took a few moments to lick the ice crystals covering the furry pads of his paws. He shook his head and tried to stand up, but he stumbled into the side of the cage and fell on his chin. He picked himself up and tried again, this time successfully. He swayed a bit, blinking. His head was lowered, his ears pressed back against his head. Mandy knew these were signs of agitation, and she willed him to be brave.

All around her, Mandy could hear the tapping of bears' claws on the concrete floors of the cells. There was an occasional huffing sound, or a snort, and the odd whimper. It was amazing to think she was surrounded by wild polar bears. Then the mother polar bear shook her massive head and stepped towards the metal bars which separated her cage from Polo's.

'Here she comes!' John Bruce said with satisfaction.

The bear was panting slightly, and with each pigeon-toed step she took, her warm breath condensed cloudily in the cold air of the cell. She looked cautious, but interested. She seemed smaller somehow than Mandy remembered.

The polar bear sniffed deeply at the air around her, again and again. She pushed her black nose between the bars of her cage, trying to reach the cub in the other pen. Polo inched closer, until he was nose to nose with the adult bear. Mandy held her breath. Would Polo recognise his mother?

The little cub let out an excited squeak, and his mother grunted in reply. Polo scratched at the bars, scraping at the metal with his sturdy little claws. He whimpered, then stood on his hindlegs, pushing against the bars with his big front feet. The iron grill shook and rattled. The mother bear stayed right where she was, pressed tight against the barrier. Her other cub lay motionless in the corner, curled into a tight, dirty white ball. She didn't stir as her brother rattled the bars of the cage again and again. Mandy's heart raced as she watched anxiously.

John Bruce operated the lever to open the bars between the two cells. As the gap appeared, Polo shuffled through. As he stood, stiff-legged, in the middle of the cell, his mother sniffed him all over, walking around him and inspecting him as if to make sure he was really there. Then Polo lay down submissively, and paddled his paws at her like a puppy. His mother began to lick his face and the wound on his chest with her long red tongue.

Mandy breathed a sigh of relief. Her fears had been groundless. Polo was back with his family. 'Just look at that, Alicia!' she breathed. 'Isn't it fantastic?'

Alicia squeezed Mandy's arm. 'Polo's mum knows exactly who he is!' she said.

'It's great!' Mr Bruce agreed. 'Good work, team!'

At that moment, the mother bear lowered herself heavily to the floor and stretched out on her side. Polo scrambled to his feet and butted his head into his mother's belly, searching for the nourishment he so badly needed. The noise of his snuffling and scrabbling woke his twin. She lifted her head, seeming hopeful, then fell back weakly. Mandy watched with growing alarm as Polo searched the furry expanse of his mother's sagging belly, rooting from teat to teat.

'That's bad news,' John Bruce muttered, frowning.

'What's the matter?' Alicia asked. 'It looks like she really wants to feed Polo.'

'The mother's milk has dried up,' Mr Bruce said flatly. 'It looks like she *can't* feed her cubs any more. That must be why the female cub is too weak to stand.'

Mandy felt her heart sink. It seemed so unfair. Polo had survived against the odds, and now he had yet another obstacle to face. He kept on trying, suckling furiously as he pushed at his mother with earnest paws. He was determined to find something to fill his empty tummy. But, finally, the exhausted mother bear bared her teeth at her cub to make him stop. She dragged herself away from him and lay down in a corner, her head on her front paws. Mandy thought she looked utterly miserable.

John Bruce stood up slowly and began to fold up the canvas stretcher he had used to carry Polo. 'We need to get them out on to the northern shores of the bay as soon as possible,' he said decisively. 'The ice will be well formed up there, and there should be plenty of hunting.' He padlocked the cage. 'Come on, girls. Let's go and investigate the possibility of flying them out.'

Mandy's heart leaped with excitement. 'You mean, we can take them out on to the bay?' she gasped.

'Now?' said Alicia, getting to her feet.

'Now,' her father repeated grimly. 'Before the weather gets too bad to fly. Come on!'

Ten

The heavy door of the jail clanged behind them. Mandy looked out into the white wilderness. She'd never seen snow like it! In the short time they had been watching the reunion between Polo and his mother, the landscape had undergone a dramatic change. The wind had picked up, forcing the snow into peaks and valleys, sculpting ice formations on any surface it could cling to. Even the bear traps had been buried. Mandy and Alicia had to scrape snow from the handle of the door before they could climb into the truck with Mr Bruce.

They drove slowly along the white road, heading for the polar sheriff's office at the airstrip. Every now and then, the headlights of huge snowploughs loomed up out of the swirling snow, making it even more difficult to see the road ahead. Mandy could feel the truck shuddering in the icy wind, and she gripped her seat tightly.

At last they pulled up outside the research building. Mandy and Alicia waited in the cab, while John Bruce went inside to see if he could arrange the flight. He was back in a few minutes, stamping the snow off his boots and looking worried as he climbed back into the driver's seat.

'No go, I'm afraid.' He shook his head, and slammed the truck door hard.

'What? Why's that?' Alicia asked, sounding alarmed.

'I can't get permission to take a helicopter up in this, lass. The whole fleet has been grounded. The bears are going to have to wait.' John Bruce wiped the snow off his face.

'How long?' Mandy asked, a feeling of desperation welling up inside her. 'How long, Mr Bruce?'

'I checked the forecast,' he told her, starting up

the engine. 'Not too long – two more days, maybe, before the wind drops. But, of course, we can't be sure.'

'Two more days!' Alicia gasped. 'But those bears need to get on to the ice sooner than that!' She looked at Mandy, her face pale.

Mandy felt desperately worried. Her dad had said that Polo would need food very soon if he was going to survive. She couldn't bear to think that the little cub might not live to explore the vast stretch of pack-ice which was waiting for the bears just a few kilometres away.

It was the longest two days Mandy could remember. The seconds crept by like minutes, the minutes like hours. Alicia and her parents did their best to make the time pass quickly. They made a giant snowman, baked a chocolate cake, and watched television. Mandy even tried to do some of her schoolwork, but she soon found herself distracted. It seemed as if the shriek and howl of the battering wind would never stop.

Her mind was constantly filled with images of Polo and his sister. Mandy could picture her beloved cub pacing his cell, growing weaker every hour.

While Adam and Emily Hope worked on their research papers, John Bruce went about his business as usual. On the second afternoon, he reported that he had driven out to Cape Churchill and seen thirty or more polar bears gathering on the ice. 'They're waiting to go,' he said. 'It won't be long now.'

'It might be too late for *our* bears,' said Mandy. She returned to the window again, as if by gazing out at the sky she could somehow will the storm to subside. The few stumpy trees along Main Street were bent double with the force of the gale. It was no use. It would be impossible to fly a helicopter in this weather, let alone carry three polar bears as passengers.

Mandy went and found her dad sitting at John Bruce's desk. He looked up and slipped an arm round her waist.

'I'm so worried about the bears,' Mandy began. 'Do you think they'll survive, Dad?'

Adam Hope smiled at her, but his eyes were solemn. 'I'm not very hopeful at the moment, Mandy,' he confessed. 'We have no way of telling how long this storm will go on – and the cubs are very weak. There is nothing we can do but wait, I'm afraid.'

So Mandy waited, and worried, and prayed for the wind to go down and for the bay to keep on freezing.

And then, on the third morning, Mandy woke up to an unusual sound – silence. The whistling and hammering of the wind had gone. She threw aside her duvet and bounded to the window. The sky was a clear, pale blue and the frozen landscape was lit by a watery sun just peeping over the horizon.

'Alicia!' Mandy yelled at the sleepy figure in the bed beside her. She ran to the top of the stairs. 'Mr Bruce! Mrs Bruce! Mum . . .' Mandy hurtled down the stairs. 'Dad!' She burst into the kitchen.

'If you're coming along with me to set those polar bears free, Mandy,' Mr Bruce said wryly, 'I suggest you change out of your pyjamas.'

'Can we really go?' Mandy gaped at him. Alicia's dad was dressed ready to leave the house.

'Sure,' John Bruce replied. 'If you get ready quickly, you can come with me.'

'Oh, thanks!' Mandy exclaimed. 'Yes, I'm coming. Of course, I'm coming. Right now?' she added.

'There isn't a moment to lose, lass,' said Mr Bruce. 'Off you go!'

Much to her annoyance, Alicia had to go to school, but she made Mandy promise to tell her everything about the trip. Then John Bruce explained that there would only be room for one other person in the helicopter, besides himself and Wayne, his co-pilot. Mandy's parents agreed to stay behind, although they would be coming to the polar jail to help load up the bears. They climbed into their rented Jeep to follow Mr Bruce and Mandy, who were in the bright yellow bear patrol truck.

Churchill's snowploughs had done a good job, and the roads were clear, so John Bruce was able to drive at top speed. The mountains of snow and ice lining the road gave Mandy the feeling she was driving through a tunnel. Even though she was thrilled to be on the way, her heart was racing with anxiety. Would it be too late to save Polo and his twin?

'Stay in the truck, Mandy,' said John Bruce as they reached the polar jail. Mr Hope pulled up next to him and waved to Mandy.

A helicopter stood on the concrete carpark, and a barrel trap had been backed up to the doors of the jail. Mandy watched as Mr Bruce's colleague Mike secured an enormous net to a sturdy metal hook on the helicopter. Meanwhile, Mandy's mum and dad joined John Bruce at the door of the polar jail, next to the barrel trap. Mr Hope was carrying a tranquillising gun. In spite of the icy air, Mandy wound down her window and put her head outside to listen to what was going on.

Mr Bruce shouted to someone inside the jail. Almost immediately, Mandy heard muffled shouts and the heavy clang of a cell door being opened. Then there was a rapid padding sound, and the barrel trap shook violently as the mother bear ran into it. Two smaller shudders indicated that her cubs had joined her. At least they were still alive, Mandy thought with relief.

Next, Mandy saw Mr Bruce open a window in the barrel, just large enough for the female to poke her head and neck out. The moment she did so, Adam Hope fired a tranquillising dart into the skin below her ear. The bear withdrew her head suddenly and vanished from view.

After a couple of minutes, the trapdoor in the barrel was cautiously opened. Mr Bruce peered in and nodded confidently. Mandy's mum helped Mike to spread out the net, as close to the barrel trap as possible. The sleeping female was dragged out by John Bruce and two of his colleagues and rolled into the net.

The cubs came stumbling out of the trap behind their mother. As they stood, dazed and blinking in the bright light, Adam Hope injected a tiny dose of tranquiliser into each one. Almost at once, the cubs flopped down on to the snow, their eyes closing.

Mr Bruce looked up and waved across to Mandy. She jumped out of the cab and ran over to the barrel trap. Polo was lying on the icy ground. His eyes were just open, but his sister's were tightly closed. Mandy's mouth felt dry. Polo looked even thinner than before.

'Can you hold one of the cubs in the helicopter, Mandy?' Mr Bruce asked as he hoisted Polo into his arms.

Mandy nodded, eager to help. She ran over to

the helicopter and clambered into the back row of seats, and John Bruce placed the dozing cub on her lap. Mandy pulled the limp furry body into her arms. She could feel Polo's ribs through his coat as she cuddled him close.

'Wayne Roberts is going to pilot us out,' Mr Bruce told her, picking up the female cub and climbing in beside her. 'You and I are in charge of these two, OK?'

'OK,' Mandy confirmed, as she shifted to make herself more comfortable under the weight of the bear cub. Adam Hope peered through the open door and grinned at Mandy. 'You OK, love?' he asked.

'Oh, yes!' said Mandy. She couldn't wait to get airborne, and take Polo and his family home.

Mr Hope said something to the pilot, and then slid the glass door shut. He waved to Mandy and gave her a thumbs-up sign. Emily Hope came up beside him, smiling encouragingly.

The blades began to whirr, and within seconds the helicopter lifted off the snowy ground. The net curled up round the mother bear, its drawstring top tightening above her until she was suspended in a giant string bag. It swung her up into the cloudless sky as if she weighed nothing at all.

'We're going to make it!' Mr Bruce looked across at Mandy and grinned. 'I think we're going to be in time to save our little family.'

They flew low over ice-bound rivers and frozen shallow ponds, heading north. Peering through the curved window, Mandy caught a glimpse of the mother bear in the huge net below. She was curled up like a dog in a basket, her eyes closed. The breeze caught at her coat and ruffled it, making it look soft pink in the morning sunlight.

The female cub slumbered fitfully at Mr Bruce's feet. Polo had closed his eyes and, from time to time, he twitched and whimpered in Mandy's arms. Mandy held on tightly to his body, and willed him to hang on. 'We're nearly there, Polo!' she whispered in his tiny ear.

'Look down there, Mandy.' Mr Bruce tapped her on the shoulder and pointed. 'Musk-ox.'

The herd of vast, shaggy creatures was gathered in a circle beside a clump of scrubby-looking pines. Their thick brown coats were almost long enough to sweep the snowy ground.

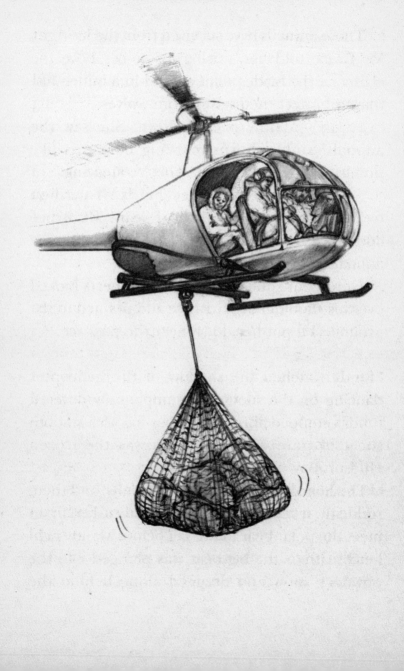

'Those animals have survived from the Ice Age,' Mr Bruce told her, raising his voice above the clatter of the blades. 'They stand in a bunch like that to protect themselves from wolves.'

'Really?' Mandy peered down. She saw the animals' stubby horns, curving outwards like prehistoric wall paintings. 'They're amazing!'

'Sometimes we see huge herds of caribou trekking north at this time of year,' Mr Bruce added. 'It always surprises me just how many animals can survive up here.'

'Here's our spot, John.' Wayne Roberts looked over his shoulder at Mr Bruce and pointed to the ground. 'I'll put her down near the pack ice.'

Mandy watched the shadow of the helicopter dancing on the snow. The lumpy, snow-covered tundra stopped abruptly, giving way to a smooth sheet of pure white ice. This was the frozen Hudson Bay.

The helicopter descended gradually, and then, suddenly, it seemed as if the ground rushed up to meet the polar bear in the net below. Mandy held her breath as the big bear was plunged into the powdery snow and dragged along behind the helicopter. The polar bear's heavy body ploughed a neat furrow through the snow. As the skids of the helicopter touched down, Mandy clutched at Polo to stop him from sliding off her lap. There was a sudden welcome quiet as the engine was silenced and the blades rattled to a stop.

John Bruce unbuckled his seat belt and slid open the door. Mandy gasped as the biting wind whipped at her hair. Mr Bruce jumped out and dragged the female cub out on to the snow. Then he lifted Polo out of Mandy's arms and laid him next to his sister. Mandy scrambled out of the helicopter and stood beside the sleepy cubs, watching as Mr Bruce approached the mother bear.

The jolt from the landing had aroused her, and she looked drowsy and bewildered as she lifted her head. When she felt the net holding her, she shook her head impatiently. Mr Bruce pulled open the neck of the net and loosened it round the polar bear's body, laying it flat around her. The bear blinked and sniffed the air, but made no attempt to get up.

'Is she going to be all right?' Mandy called.

'I should think so. She's just a bit dazed,' Mr

Bruce replied. 'OK, Wayne, you can bring the cubs to me.'

Mandy helped Wayne to carry first one, and then the other cub over to where their mother lay. The big bear was breathing hard, and trying to rise. She rolled her eyes angrily.

Moving quickly, John Bruce placed a cub on either side of her. 'Back now,' he warned. 'Let's move, she'll be on her feet soon.'

They ran to the safety of the helicopter and jumped in. Mandy pushed the hood of her jacket back from her head and wiped the condensation from the window. She was desperate to see the bears wake up.

'Don't take off just yet, Wayne, will you?' Mr Bruce called to his co-pilot. 'Let's hang around a bit and watch.'

Mandy's heart thudded in her chest. This was it!

Very slowly, the mother bear climbed to her feet. She stumbled about, finding her balance and looking around her warily. Then she sniffed at the net, patting it with her massive front paw. The cubs nudged against her, fully awake now and wanting attention. But their mother was alert to something else, her sleek nose raised to the breeze. She snapped at Polo, who was trying to push his nose into her belly.

'I hope they find plenty to eat out there,' said Mandy.

'Don't worry, lass,' John Bruce said beside her. 'They'll find food soon enough.'

As if on cue, the mother bear began moving in the direction of the pack ice. Her head was high, and her nose worked furiously. The scent of food was on the wind – and she began to pick up speed. Lifting her shaggy, pigeon-toed paws, she streaked across the ice.

Polo and his sister did their best to keep up. They went after her, as fast as their small legs could carry them, leaping towards freedom, and food. The clean, cold air and endless empty spaces seemed to have given them a burst of energy, as if they knew they were going to be all right.

'There they go!' said John Bruce with satisfaction.

Mandy felt a surge of overwhelming relief. She wanted to shout for joy. Instead, she leaned over and hugged Mr Bruce. 'I'm so glad,' she said simply. 'I'm so happy for them.'

'We'd better be starting for home, chief,' Wayne told them, tapping the face of his watch. 'There'll be plenty more bears waiting for this chopper.'

'You're right.' John Bruce nodded, settling back and buckling his seat belt. 'Let's get going.'

As the helicopter soared into the cloudless sky with the empty net dangling beneath it, Mandy took a last look at the polar bears. The little family was trotting confidently across the ice. Narrow cracks criss-crossed the vast expanse of frozen water which hugged the Hudson Bay coastline. In places the pack ice reared up in jagged peaks, forced upward by the turbulent waters below. Where the wind gusted over the surface, the newly-fallen snow rose in smoky swirls. Looking like miniature toys against the vast white backdrop, the bears began to run, and Mandy felt her happiness well up inside her.

'Goodbye, little bear,' Mandy murmured. As the shadow of the helicopter flickered over him, Polo looked up. Mandy gazed down at his beloved little face with the coal-black button nose. 'Goodbye, Polo.'